Paingod and Other Delusions

Paingod and Other Delusions

Harlan Ellison

© Copyright 1965, 1975 by Harlan Ellison
© Copyright 1983 by The Kilimanjaro Corporation
First e-reads publication 1999
www.e-reads.com
ISBN 0-7592-2994-5

Other works by Harlan Ellison

also available in e-reads editions

The first edition of this book was dedicated to a friend of fourteen years' brotherhood. He is now a friend of twenty-nine years' shared joys and agonies. If anything, this rededication is even more appropriate, tagged as it is for

ROBERT SILVERBERG

Table of Contents

Paingod and Other Delusions

Acknowledgements

"Paingod" (in a slightly abridged version) originally appeared in *Fantastic*, June 1964; copyright © 1964 by Ziff-Davis Publishing Company. Copyright reassigned to Author 6 January 1981. Copyright © 1981 by The Kilimanjaro Corporation.

"'Repent, Harlequin!' Said the Ticktockman" originally appeared in *Galaxy*, December 1965; copyright © 1966 by Harlan Ellison.

"The Crackpots" originally appeared in *IF: Worlds of Science Fiction*, June 1956; copyright © 1956 by Quinn Publishing Company. Copyright reassigned to Author 25 March 1975. Copyright © 1975 by Harlan Ellison.

"Sleeping Dogs" originally appeared in *Analog Science Fiction/Fact*, October 1974; copyright © 1974 by Harlan Ellison.

"Bright Eyes" originally appeared in *Fantastic*, April 1965; copyright © 1965 by Ziff-Davis Publishing Company. Copyright reassigned to Author 10 March 1981. Copyright © 1981 by The Kilimanjaro Corporation.

"The Discarded" (under the title "The Abnormals") originally appeared in *Fantastic*, April 1959; copyright © 1959 by Ziff-Davis Publishing Company.

New Introduction

Your Basic Crown of Thorns

O ne night, some years ago, maybe five or six, I woke up in the darkness and saw words burning bright-red on the ceiling of my bedroom.

ARE YOU AWARE OF HOW MUCH
PAIN THERE IS IN THE WORLD?

I crawled out of the rack and felt my way through the house to my office, sat down at the typewriter, put on the light and—still asleep—typed the words on paper. I went back to bed and forgot all about it. That night I had programmed my dreams for a Sergio Leone spaghetti western with score by Morricone. No cartoon, no short subjects.

The next morning, coffee cup in hand, I went to my typewriter and found the question waiting for me, all alone on a sheet of yellow foolscap. Rhetorical. Of *course* I knew how much pain there was in the world ... *is* in the world.

But I couldn't quite bring myself to ripping the sheet off the roller and getting on with what I should have been working at. I sat and stared at it for the longest time.

1

Understand something: I am not a humanitarian. I distrust selfless philanthropists and doers of good deeds. When you discover that the black natives of Lamborene hated Schweitzer, you begin to suspect noble individuals have some secret need in them to be loved, to look good in others' eyes, to succor themselves or dissipate their guilts with benevolent gestures. Rather than the sanctimonious bullshit of politicians about "the good people of this fair state," I would joyously vote for any candidate who had the courage to stand up and say, "Look, I'm going to steal from you. I'm going to line my pockets and those of my friends, but I'm not going to steal *too* much. But in the deal I'll give you better roads, safer schools, better education, and a happier condition of life. I'm not going to do it out of compassion or dedication to the good people of this fair state; I'm going to do it because if I *do* these things, you'll elect me again and I can steal a little bit more." That joker has my vote, no arguments.

(Rule of thumb: whenever you hear a politician call it "the United States of America" instead of simply "the U.S."—you know he's bullshitting you. It's like the convoluted syntax of college textbooks. When they start writing in a prolix manner that makes you read a paragraph seven times to get the message *See Dick and Jane run, oh oh oh!* you know someone is trying to flummox you. Same for politicians; if they start running a fast ramadoolah past you, instead of speaking simply and directly, they're trying to weasel. This lesson in good government comes to you through the courtesy of a man who was snookered by Eugene McCarthy *and* George McGovern.)

So what I'm trying to tell you is that I'm last in the line of noble, unselfish, golden humanitarians. What I do for the commonweal I do for *myself*. I am a selfish sonofabitch who contributes to "good causes" because I feel shitty if I don't. But if the truth be told, I'm the same as you: the deaths of a hundred thousand flood victims in some banana republic doesn't touch me one one-millionth as much as the death of my dog did. If you get wiped out on a freeway somewhere and I don't know you personally, I may go tsk-tsk, but the fact that I haven't had a good bowel movement in two days is more painful to me.

So those words burning on my ceiling really threw me.

They really got to me.

I had them printed on big yellow cards so they'd pop, and I started giving them to friends. I had one framed for my office. It's up on the wall to the right of my typewriter as I sit here telling you about it.

But if I'm not this terrific *concerned* human being, what's it all in aid of? Well, it's in aid of my coming to terms with my own mortality, something that'll happen to all of you if it hasn't already. And it speaks to what this collection of stories is all about, in a way. So we'll talk about pain.

Here are a few different kinds of pain I think are worthy of our attention.

2

The other night I had dinner with a good friend, a woman writer whom I've known for about ten years. Though we've never had a romantic relationship, I love her dearly and care about her: she's a *good* person, and a talented writer, and those two qualities put her everlastingly on my list of When You Need Help, Even in the Dead of Night, I'm on Call. Over dinner, we talked about an anguish she has been experiencing for a number of years. She's afraid of dying alone and unloved.

Some of you are nodding in understanding. A few of you are smiling. The former understand pain, the latter are assholes. Or very lucky. We've *all* dreaded that moment when we pack it in, get a fast rollback of days and nights, and realize we're about to go down the hole never having belonged to anyone. If you've never felt it, you're either an alien from far Arcturus or so insensitive your demise won't matter. Or very lucky.

Her problem is best summed up by something Theodore Sturgeon once said: "There's no absence of love in the world, only worthy places to put it." My friend gets involved with guys who do her in. Not all her fault. Some of it is—we're never wholly victims, we help construct the tiger traps filled with spikes—but not all of it. She's vulnerable. While not naïve, she *is* innocent. And that's a dangerous but laudable capacity: to wander through a world that can be very uncaring and amorally cruel, and still be astonished at the way the sunlight catches the edge of a coleus leaf. Anybody puts her down for that has to go through me first.

So she keeps trying, and the ones with long teeth sense her vulnerability and they move in for the slow kill. (That's evil: only the human predator destroys slowly, any decent hunting animal rips out the throat and feeds, and that's that. The more I see of people, the better I like animals.)

She is a woman who needs a man. There are men who need a good woman. There's nothing sexist in saying that, it's a condition of the animal. (And just so I don't get picketed by Gay Lib, there are men who need a good man and women who need a good woman. There are also men who need a good chicken and women who need a big dog, and that's nobody's business but their own, you get my meaning, so let's cut the crap and move on.) Everybody needs to belong to somebody. Sometime. For an hour, a day, a year, forever ... it's all the same. And when you've paid dues on a bunch of decades without having made the proper linkup, you come to live with a pain that is a dull ache, unlocalized, suffusing every inch of your skin and throbbing like a bruise down on the bone.

What to tell her, what to say? There's nothing. I'll try to find her someone who cares, but it's a pain she'll have to either overcome by guerrilla attacks on the singles bars and young-marrieds' parties, or learn to love herself sufficiently well that she becomes more accessible to the men she's turning off by unspoken

3

words and invisible vibes. People sense the pain, and they shy away from it, because they've felt it themselves, and they don't want to get contaminated. When you need a job and hunger for one openly, you never get hired because they smell desperation on you like panther sweat.

But it's a pain you can't ignore. I can't ignore.

Here's another one.

What follows is one of hundreds of letters I get from readers. I hate getting mail, because I don't have the time to answer it, and I get a lot of it— probably due to writing introductions like this where I expose my viscera— but more of that and what Avram Davidson says about it later on—and most of the time I send out a form letter, otherwise I wouldn't have time to write stories. But occasionally I get a letter that simply cannot be ignored. This is one of them.

I won't use the young woman's name for reasons of libel that will become clear as you read the letter. The story to which she makes reference is titled "Lonelyache" and it appears in my collection I HAVE NO MOUTH AND I MUST SCREAM [Pyramid Books, 1974]. It is about a man who comes to unhappy terms with his own overpowering guilt about being a loveless individual. The "Discon" reference is to the World SF Convention held on Labor Day 1974 in Washington, D.C.

Dear Harlan:

We spoke briefly at Discon concerning reading sf to the mentally ill—your sf among others'. Something happened the other day that I thought might interest you.

I am presently working in the one medical-surgical building that—has. Since most of my patients are in here for only very short stays, there has not been much opportunity for me to continue the reading/therapy that I had been doing in another, quieter building. (Also, having IV bottles and bouncing EKG's to baby-sit leaves little time for other pastimes, however therapeutic.) (And furthermore, I'm working midnight shift now—which cuts down somewhat on people interested in being read to.)

Anyway. In this madhouse of a building we have, among wards intended to hold up to twenty-five, one which cannot house more than seven: Ward 6A; otherwise known as Wounded Knee (from a time when we had five fractured patellas up here at once). A fracture ward, as it were, which also houses diabetics being newly-regulated, and staph infections, and new heart attacks who're healing. Rather a quiet place as contrasted to most of this madhouse (pardon unintentional pun), and since I came back from Discon, my very own ward (on nights).

We have up here at present a patient who has put more employees of various sorts out on compensation for various injuries of various sorts than any other patient in the hospital.

The reason for this is hardly any fault of hers: the fault lies with the aforementioned employees, who worked constantly (maybe unwittingly, but that doesn't excuse them) to drive her a good deal more insane than she ever was to begin with. The syndrome is easily described. A) Some facet of our enlightened state hospital system (the Earth should only swallow it) enrages/tortures an already hurting mind to the point where it can no longer control itself and the person attacks the first thing that comes to hand. Eventually, an employee steps in to halt the mayhem, and gets mayhemmed himself. B) The word goes around from staff to staff, from staff to patients, eventually is voiced right in front of the sick person involved: "That one is nuts, will kill you if you turn your back, goes bananas at the drop of a hat, etc. ad nauseam ..." C) The person thinks, "I haven't been too well lately, these are attendants and nurses and such, they say I'm crazy; who am I to prove them wrong? So I'll be crazy, I'll attack everything in sight ..." and so it goes, and the ugly circle turns on itself. Follows thereupon much Thorazine, many camisoles, long hours in seclusion which do no one any good. Things get worse.

As it was on the night of this past July 4th. The lady who is now one of "MY PEOPLE" was in seclusion—as usual—on a third-floor ward. It was hot. No one would bring her a drink of water. Also, her room stank—as might have been expected: no one would take her out to the john, she had long since stopped asking, and had used the floor. The stench, and the heat, and her thirst all combined, and she rose up and determined to go OUT. Naturally, as she later explained it to me, they would not let her out. So she reached out, heaved at the screening that she had been yanking on for the past five years, managed to detach it, and went OUT. Three floors down.

Naturally, she had fractures. The right humerus, the right tibia and fibula, a refracture of the left tibia and a new one of the left ankle. (Amazingly, that was all—no pelvic or spinal involvement.) She was sent up to my ward. It was very interesting up here for a while: she insisted that she was fine, that her legs hurt a little but she wanted to take a walk, that was what she had come out for, anyway ... . What do you say to something like that? I cried a lot, and held her down. The next day I was transferred to another building, where they needed a nurse, so they said.

After much screaming and yelling at the chief of Nursing Services, I managed to get out of the nothing building where they sent me—a building in no need whatsoever of another nurse, where the only really worthwhile thing to do was to read to the patients—and came back to the Med-Surg building. It took me a month.

When I got back, I found matters somewhat improved. The day nurse on this ward is a good friend of mine, a very highly skilled lady who got something like a 99 in her psychiatric nursing course, and deserved more. She was not afraid of this patient, and had been doing constant therapy on her. It was working. The patient was calmer than she had been, was being weaned off the 4000 mg/day of Thorazine that her building had had her on (500 mg/day is enough to quiet just about anyone, but a tolerance had built up), she was beginning to look around and see things, to form relationships with people (she was schizophrenic, and was actually reaching out ... incredible). She still had relapses, incidents of going for people, of throwing things, but they were abortive. She was getting better.

Some time passed ... she continued to improve. I got taken off my job for a while to go through the hospital's orientation program, came back again for a little while, found her doing well, took a few days' leave for Discon, came back, found her still getting better—and then everything fell in on me—on her—rather suddenly.

This requires a small digression. We have on this ward, on the evening shift, an idiot. It has the letters R.N. after its name, but don't let it fool you: a nurse it ain't. This person delights in tormenting the patients verbally, and not getting caught at it. God knows I've tried, but I must walk too heavy or something. On this particular night she told the patient that the day nurse (whom the patient loved dearly, and who was having her turn in orientation) was never, never coming back again. Are there words foul enough for such a person? Well ...

I came on at 12, checked my ward, found things quiet: the patient in question resting in bed, awake. I went to her, checked her casts (arm and both legs), spoke to her: she didn't answer. This was par for the course, so I wished her good night and went away.

About 1:30 I heard something go crack! and then heard glass shatter on the floor. By the time I was standing up, something went thud! and by the time I reached the door of the office, so had my patient. She was out of her bed, teetering on her casts, with a big sharp piece of glass in her uncasted left hand. The hand was bleeding a little, but that was not what concerned me. This lady was no amateur, no wristslasher; she would bend her head back to cut her throat. She was faster than I was: also somewhat larger. (Picture it if you will, Harlan: 160 lbs. of her, about six feet tall: 104 lbs. of me, 5'6": and she has the glass. Who wins the wrestling match? You can't use aikido holds on someone with three casted extremities. I can't, anyway.) (Not when the fourth is flailing glass—and it's my patient.)

So we stood there, and I looked up (a mile or so, it seemed) and said, "What's the matter?" and she said, "Pat's not coming back, (the R.N.) said so, and I don't want to believe her: but if it's true, then I want to be dead. And if it's not true, look at me, look how easily someone made me go crazy! I ought to be dead."

Everything useful or therapeutic I had ever learned, heard or read went shoosh! out of my head, leaving me tabula rasa, as the saying goes, and feeling hopeless. And I opened my mouth, knowing full well that nothing worthwhile would come out, and the tail of my eye caught sight of an idea, sitting on top of a pile of books on calligraphy that I had brought with me: a copy of I HAVE NO MOUTH AND I MUST SCREAM. I said, "Come on in, sit down, let's talk about it. I have something here that may interest you." And we sat down, and I took my life in my hands and read her "Lonelyache."

You proclaimed the story to be therapy in the introduction, of course. I have often wondered after reading it just how far your own experience paralleled it. Merely clinical interest— all the wondering went out of me that night. I was watching my lady.

About halfway through she put the glass aside and shut her eyes and listened. I shook and kept reading.

When it was nearly finished, I panicked: the ending was too downkey: the protagonist commits suicide! I didn't know if I could turn her mood upward again.

I finished it, and she looked at me hard for a few seconds, and I said, "Well, what does it do for you?" She was quiet a moment, and then said, "He wanted to be brave on the way out, didn't he?"

6

"I think so," I said.

She thought some more. "But he did go out."

I nodded. It was all that was left in me: I was getting the beginnings of Oh-God-I-Did-the-Wrong-Thing! *and I was holding hard to keep it from showing.*

"Is that the only way to go, then?" she asked, and oh! the despair. I wanted to cry and couldn't. I said, "But consider first: why did he go?"

"Because he was all alone." And she looked at me, and fed me the straight line I had been praying for: "I'm all alone too, though—aren't I?"

"Do you think you're all alone?"

She looked at me, and at the glass, and at me again, and stood up rocking on her casts again. She tossed the answer off so casually: "No, I guess not." She clumped back to her room, got back in bed, and rolled herself up in the covers and went to sleep. So casually.

So even if you weren't here in the body, Harlan, you helped. No telling whether this will happen again, or how many times, or what might trigger it, but this time you helped. I thank you for having the guts to put your own fear and loneliness down on paper and then allowing it to be published: it takes courage. And has done someone some good.

Thought you might like to know.

That's another kind of pain, and it's real, and if that letter didn't hurt you where you hurt best, then *nothing* in this book will touch you, and maybe you ought to be volunteering for something like the Genocide Corps in Brazil.

Here's another pain that crushes.

I went to Driver Survival School last Saturday. I'd gotten a ticket I didn't deserve (are there any other kinds?) and the judge at my trial suggested if I wanted to take a day's worth of traffic school the ticket would be dismissed. So I did the deed.

Traffic Survival School, what a rip-off, I thought. Cynical and smartass like the other fifty people booked for that day. Seven and a half hours of bullshit from some redneck cop.

Sure.

But something happened. Something that turned me around. You've got to know, I don't like cops. It's a gut reaction I've had since I was a tiny tot. My first encounter with the Man is recorded in a story called "Free with This Box" and you'll be able to read it in GENTLEMAN JUNKIE. The story was written a long time ago, and the event happened even longer ago, but the reaction is as fresh in me as if it had happened yesterday. So I went with a snarl on my lips and a loathing for the Laws that Bonnie and Clyde would have envied.

But the two California Highway Patrol officers who lectured the class were sharp and open and knew they had a captive audience, and course-corrected for it. But still everyone in the room was cynical, taking it all as a lark, dragged by the waste of having to spend a dynamite Saturday in a small room in the Sportsmen's Lodge, sitting on a hard chair and learning the whys&wherefores of the new California U-turn law.

Until they showed the obligatory highway safety horror film.

I've seen them before, so have you. Endless scenes of maimed and crushed men and women being crowbarred out of burning wrecks; women with their heads split open like pomegranates, their brains on the Tarmac; guys who'd been hit by trains at crossings, legs over here, arms over there; shots of cars that demonstrate the simple truth that the human body is only a baggie filled with fluid—the tuck&roll interiors evenly coated with blood and meat. And it sickens you, and you turn your head away, and sensitive stomachs heave, and no one makes clever remarks, and you want to puke. But it somehow has no more effect in totality than the 7:00 News with film of burned Vietnamese babies. You never think it'll happen to you.

Until they came to the final scene of the film, and it was so hairy even the Cal Highway officers grew weak: a six-year-old black kid had been hit by a car. Black ghetto neighborhood. Hundreds of people lining the street rubbernecking. Small shape covered by a blanket in the middle of the street. Cops all over the place. According to the film it wasn't the driver's fault, kid had run out from between parked cars, driver hadn't had time to stop, centerpunched the kid doing 35.

Shot of the car. A tiny dent. Not enough to even Earl Scheib it. Small shape under a blanket.

Then they brought the mother out to identify the kid. Two men supporting her between them. They staggered forward with her and a cop lifted the edge of the blanket.

They must have had someone there with a directional mike. I got every breath, every moan, every whisper of air. Oh my God. The sound of that woman's scream. The pain. From out of the center of the earth. No human throat was ever meant to produce such a terrible sound. She collapsed, just sank away like limp meat between the supporting men. And the film ended. And I still heard that scream.

It's five days later as I write this. I cannot block that scream from my mind. I never will. I now drive more slowly, I now fasten my safety belt, I now take no chances. I have always been a fast driver, some say a crazy driver; though I've never had an accident and used to race sports cars, I always thought I was a fucking Barney Oldfield. No more. Chuckle if you will, friends, but I'm on the wagon. And that wagon gonna move *very* carefully. I don't *ever* want to hear that scream outside my head.

Are you aware of how much pain there is in the world?

Yeah, I'm aware. Now. Because I've been writing for eighteen years and I keep getting these letters, and I keep listening to people, and at times it's too much to handle. If you don't know what I'm talking about, go read Nathanael West's MISS LONELYHEARTS.

And so I write these introductions, what my friend and the brilliant writer Avram Davidson calls "going naked in the world." Avram wrote me recently and, in the course of taking me to task for something he believed I had done wrong, he more-than-mildly castigated me for dumping it all on paper. Well, he's not the first, and from time to time I've considered never writing another of these self-examinations. But Irwin Shaw said, "A man does not write one novel at a time or one play at a time or even one quatrain at a time. He is engaged in the long process of putting his whole life on paper. He is on a journey and he is reporting in: 'This is where I think I am and this is what this place looks like today.'"

This report, then, is about pain. The subject is very much with me. My mother had another heart attack, and the general topic of mortality obsesses me these days. We will all die, no reprieve. A beautiful young lady of my acquaintance, who happens to be an accomplished astrologer, told me (though she knows I don't believe in astrology) that my chart says I'm going to die by being beheaded. Terrific remark. She told it to me one night when we were out on a date, and she was surprised that I turned out to be no goddam good in bed that night.

Well, she needn't have been so surprised; I know I'm going to buy the farm one day, sooner or later depending on how much I run my mouth in dangerous situations. But it isn't death that bothers me, it's dying alone.

So I think about pain, and I present you with this group of stories that say a little something about what I've learned on the subject. They may not be terribly deep or illuminating, just some random thoughts I've had through the years. A few of them seem funny, and they were intended so because I think the only things that get us through the pain are laughter and the promise of love to come. At least the possibility of it. But each one of them has some special pain in it, and I urge you to seek it out, through the chuckles and the bug-eyed aliens and the what-if furniture that makes these stories and not sermons.

Because there's only one thing that links us as human beings: the universality of our pain and the commonality of our need to go out bravely.

Harlan Ellison
9 November '74

Introduction to First Edition

SPERO MELIORA:

From the Vicinity of Alienation

This is my eleventh book. (It should have been thirteen, counting the one I did under a pseudonym for a schlock publisher because I needed the money some years ago, but number twelve was a false start Avram Davidson and myself wish had never happened and fortunately never got into print, and thirteen is a book of short stories no one seems constitutionally capable of publishing, and which seems well on its way to becoming an "underground classic" for those who have read it in manuscript form.) That doesn't seem too bad, for thirty years; twenty of which were spent in learning on which end of this particular body the head was attached.

Very nearly all of the past ten books have had some sort of introduction or prologue by myself. I have the feeling it is necessary to know what a writer stands for, in what he believes, what it takes to make him bleed, before a reader should be asked to care about what the writer has written. This is patently foolish. B. Traven writes eloquently, feelingly, brilliantly, yet he is an unknown quantity. Wilde's life contradicts most of what he wrote. Shaw and Dickens and Stendhal were virtually anonymous in their seminal, important years, yet what they wrote remains keen and true and valid. Granted, the philosophy of "love me, love my writing" is *my* problem. Still, it is the one to which I pander, and so each of my books has had some viscera-revealing treatise at the opening, from which the usual reader reaction has been total revulsion and a mind-boggling reeling-back in disbelief. I have the unseemly habit of going naked into the world. It comes from a seamy desire on my part not only to be a Great Writer, but to Be Adored as well.

There is no introduction this time.

I'm tired.

This is my first book in over two years. (In early 1962 I came out to Hollywood, as part of a package deal that involved dismembering a marriage and fracturing a small but intense group of lives. I've been here over three years, as this is written, and I've been busy making a decent living in television and feature films to do much book work. And I cry a lot.)

I hit thirty-one last May; I turned around, and I'd grown up. I knew Santa Claus was a winehead who spent the other eleven months sopping up watery chicken soup with brown bread in a Salvation Army kitchen; the Easter Bunny was only Welsh Rarebit mispronounced; "good women" exist in their idyllic state mostly in weak novels by Irving Wallace, John O'Hara, Fannie Hurst, and Leon Urine (my misspell, not the typesetter's); Marilyn Monroe, Camus, and JFK got cut off in their prime, and the eggsucking monsters who buried those three Civil Rights workers twenty-one feet down are running loose; and the sense of wonder has been relegated to buying old comic books and catching *The Shadow* on Sunday radio, trying to find out where that innocence of childhood or nature went.

So there is no introduction. It has made this book incredibly belated in appearing already. Seven times I tried to start an introduction to it, while Don Bensen (an incredibly patient, longsuffering, extremely fine editor) was stunned by the hammers of deadlines, publishers, schedules, and irresponsible authors. And seven times I came to ass-grinding halts.

The first few times it was a compendium of bitter, cynical comment on writing for the science fiction field. Then there was a lighthearted rollicking essay on Life in Our Times, but by the time I had hit the thirty-six ball-less wonders who watched Catherine Genovese get knifed to death in New York, my rollick was a bit strained. So I attempted a more serious assaying of the contemporary scene. It touched on such matters as the afternoon I was called a Communist by the bag-boy in the Thriftimart because I objected to the Goldwater pamphlets at point-of-sale; the impertinence and nosiness of credit checks for job applications or credit cards; the shocking bastardization of news media and lack of responsibility thereof; the fetish for style and luxury, not safety, in new cars ... .

Oh, I went the route.

11

And when I was done, it took three close friends to keep me from dashing into the bathroom and opening an important vein with the new beep-beep Krona edge.

So I tried a sixth attempt. A personal statement about how crummy it was writing for television, and seeing your best work masticated and grab-assed and garbaged-out by no-talents afraid of their shadows. But that was only a repeat of a speech I made at the World SF Convention last Labor Day, and my attorney warned me if I put it into print (instead of playing it via tape at parties), I'd be sued for roughly eleven million beans. So there was a seventh attempt, in which I commented sagely on the stories in this book.

But let's face it, friends, this book simply ain't gonna change the course of Western Civilization, and Orville Prescott is too busy simpering over Updike to find time for a paperback novelist, so what the hell.

So there is no introduction to this book.

There are some pretty fair science fiction and fantasy stories here, and one or two I particularly like because they say something more than The Mutants Is Coming; if Bensen can wangle the space away from Pyramid's advertising department to cut the latest notification of a Taylor Caldwell or Louis Nizer offering, there may or may not be a photo of me on the back of the book (should you happen to be the sort of good-looking broad who digs writing to weary authors, but need to know they aren't hunchbacked lepers before committing yourself); there is a nice cover; and a fair-traded price.

More than that you can't expect.

After all, Golding doesn't introduce *his* books. Bellow doesn't introduce *his* books. Ike Asimov has proved his virility enough for *all* us science fiction writers. And Ayn Rand is better at karate than *all* of us. So forgive the omission this time. I'll catch you next time around.

You wouldn't have liked an introduction, anyway.

I tend to pomposity in them.

Harlan Ellison
Hollywood, 1965

Late in March of 1965, I was compelled to join twenty-five thousand others, from all corners of the United States, who marched on the then-bastion of bigotry, the then-capitol of corruption, Montgomery, Alabama (though South Boston now holds undisputed title to the designation, Montgomery is still no flowerbed of racial sanity) (but the myth of the "liberal" North sure got the hell shot out of it by the Southies from Irish-redneck Boston).

I was part of the human floodtide they called a "freedom march" that was trying to tell Governor George Wallace that Alabama was not an island, that it was part of the civilized universe, that though we came from New York and California and Illinois and South Dakota we were not "outside agitators," we were fellow human beings who shared the same granfalloon called "Americans," and we were seeking dignity and civil rights for a people shamefully bludgeoned and mistreated for over two centuries. It was a walk through the country of the blind. I've written about it at length elsewhere.

But now it's ten years later and yesterday a friend of mine's sixty-five-year-old mother got mugged and robbed in broad daylight by two black girls. It's ten years later and a girl I once loved very deeply got raped repeatedly, at knife-point, in the back seat of her own car in an empty lot behind a bowling alley in the San Fernando Valley by a black dude who kept at her for seven hours. It's ten years later and Martin Luther King is dead and Super Fly is alive, and what am I to say to Doris Pitkin Buck, who lost her dear and magical Richard on the streets

13

of Washington, D.C., to a pack of black killers who chose to stomp to death a man in his eighties for however much stash-money he might have been carrying?

Do I say to that friend of mine: when they went to drag the Mississippi swamps for the bodies of the civil rights workers Chaney, Schwerner, and Goodman, they dredged up the bodies of sixteen black men who had been cavalierly murdered and dumped in the muck, and no one even gave a damn, the newspapers didn't even make much of a note of it, that it was the accepted way to handle an "uppity nigger" in the South? Do I say that and hope I've said something rational?

Do I say to that girl I loved: every time you see a mocha-colored maid or waitress it means her great-great-grandmother was a sexual pin cushion for some plantation Massa', that rape and indentured bed service was taken for granted for two hundred years and if it was refused there was always a stout length of cordwood to change the girl's thinking? Do I say that and hope I've drawn a reasonable parallel?

Do I tell brave and talented Doris Buck, who never hurt anyone in her life, that we're paying dues for what our ancestors did, that we're reaping the terrible crop of pain and evil and murder committed in the name of White Supremacy, that white men rob and rape and steal and kill as well as black, but that blacks are poorer, more desperate, more frustrated, angrier? Do I say that and hope to stop her tears with logic?

Why the hell do we expect a nobility of blacks that whites never possessed?

Of course I don't say that pack of simple-minded platitudes. Personal pain is incapable of spontaneous remission in the presence of loss. I say nothing.

But my days of White Liberal Guilt are gone. My days of championing whole classes and sexes and pigmentations of people are gone. The Sixties are gone, and we live in the terrible present, where death and guilt don't mix. Now I come, after all these years, to the only position that works: each one on his or her own merits, black/white/yellow/brown. Not all Jews are money-gouging kikes, but some are. Not all blacks are slavering rapists, but some are. Not all Puerto Ricans are midnight second-storey spicks, but some are.

And we come to the question again and again, what kind of a god is it that permits such misery ... are we truly cast in his image, such an image of cruelty and rapaciousness ... were we put here really to suffer such torment? Let the Children of God answer that one with something other than no-brain jingoism. Mark Twain said, "If one truly believes there is an all-powerful Deity, and one looks around at the condition of the universe, one is led inescapably to the conclusion that God is a malign thug." That's the quote that caused me to write "The Deathbird." It's a puzzle I cannot reason out.

I doubt. I have always doubted, since the day I read in the Old Testament—the word of God, remember—that there was only Adam and Eve and Cain and Abel, and then Cain got married. To whom? To Eve? Then don't tell me what a no-no incest is.

Isaac Asimov assures me it's a rational universe, predicated on sanity and order. Yeah? Well, tell me about God. Tell me who He is, why He allows the foulest hyenas of our society to run amuck while decent men and women cower in terror behind Fox locks and Dictograph systems. Tell me about Him. Equate theology with the world in which we live, with William

Calley and Kitty Genovese and the people who keep their kids out of school because the new textbooks dare to say Humans are clever descendants of the Ape. No? Having some trouble? Getting ready to write me a letter denouncing me as the Antichrist? "God in his infinite wisdom," you say? Faith, you urge me? I have faith ... in people, not Gods.

But perhaps belief is not enough. Perhaps doubt serves the cause more honestly, more boldly. If so, I offer by way of faith

Paingod

Tears were impossible, yet tears were his heritage. Sorrow was beyond him, yet sorrow was his birthright. Anguish was denied him; even so, anguish was his stock in trade. For Trente, there was no unhappiness; nor was there joy, concern, discomfort, age, time, feeling.

And this was as the Ethos had planned it.

For Trente had been appointed by the Ethos—the race of somewhere/somewhen beings who morally and ethically ruled the universes—as their Paingod. To Trente, who knew neither the tug of time nor the crippling demands of the emotions, fell the forever task of dispensing pain and sorrow to the myriad multitudes of creatures that inhabited the universes. Whether sentient or barely capable of the feeblest unicellular reaction-formation, Trente passed along from his faceted cubicle invisible against the backdrop of the changing stars, unhappiness and misery in proportions too complexly arrived at to be verbalized.

He was Paingod for the universes, the one who dealt out the tears and the anguish and the soul-wrenching terrors that blighted life from its first moment to its last. Beyond age, beyond death, beyond feeling—lonely

16

and alone in his cubicle—Trente went about his business without concern or pause.

Trente was not the first Paingod, there had been others. They had come before, not too many of them, but a few, and why they no longer held their post was a question Trente had never asked. He was the chosen one from a race that lived almost indefinitely, and his job was to pass along the calibrated and measured dollops of melancholy as prescribed by the Ethos. It involved no feeling and no concern, only attention to duty. It was his position, and it was his obligation. How peculiar it was that he felt concern, after all this time.

It had begun so long before—and of time he had no conception—that the only marking date with validity was that in the great ocean soon to become the Gobi Desert, paramecia had become more prevalent than amoebae. It had grown in him through the centimetered centuries as layers and layers of forever settled down like mist to form the stratum of the past.

Now, it was now.

Despite the strange ache in his nerve-gland, his *central* nerve-gland; despite the progressive dulling of his eye globes; despite the mad thoughts that spit and stuttered through his triple-domed cerebrum, thoughts of which he knew he was incapable; despite all this, Trente performed his now functions as he was required.

He dispensed unbearable anguish to the residents of a third-power planet in the Snail Cluster, supportable agony to a farm colony that had sprung up on Jacopettii U; incredible suffering to a parentless spider-child on Hiydyg IX; and relentless torment to a blameless race of mute aborigines on a nameless, arid planet circling a dying sun of the 707 System.

And through it all, Trente suffered for his charges.

What could not be, was. What could not come to pass, had. The soulless, emotionless, regimented creature that the Ethos had named Paingod, had contracted a sickness. Concern. He cared. At last, after centuries too filed away to unearth and number, Trente had reached a Now in which he could no longer support his acts.

The physical manifestations of his mental upheaval were numerous. His oblong head throbbed and his eye globes were dulling, a little more each decade; the interlinked duodenal ulcers so necessary to his endocrine system's normal function had begun to misfire like faulty plugs in an old car; the thwack! of his salamander tail had grown weaker, indicating his motor responses were feebler. Trente—who had always been considered rather a handsome example of his race—had slowly come to look forlorn, weary, even a touch pathetic.

And he sent down woe to an armored, flying creature with a mite-sized brain on a dark planet at the edge of the Coalsack; he dispatched fear and trembling to a smokelike wraith that was the only visible remains of a great race, which had learned to dispense with its bodies centuries before, in the sun known as Vertel; he conscientiously winged terror and unhappiness and misery and sadness to a group of murdering pirates, a clique of shrewd politicians and a brothelful of unregenerate whores—all on a fifth-power planet of the White Horse Constellation.

Stopped alone there, in the night of space, his mind spiraling now for the first time down a strange and disquieting chamber of thought, Trente twisted within himself. I was selected because I lacked the certain difficulties I now manifest. What is this torment? What is this unpleasant, unhappy, unrelenting feeling that gnaws at me, tears at me, corrupts my thoughts, colors darkly my every desire? Am I going mad? Madness is beyond my race; it is a something we have never known. Have I been at this post too long, have I failed in my duties? If there was a God stronger than the God that I am, or a God stronger than the Ethos Gods, then I would appeal to that God. But there is only silence and the night and the stars, and I'm alone, so alone, so God all alone here, doing what I must, doing my best.

And then, finally: I must know. I must *know!*

... while he spun a fiber of melancholy down to a double-thoraxed insect-creature on Io, speared with dread a blob of barely sentient mud on Acaras III, pain-goaded into suicide an electrical-wave being capable of producing exquisite 15-toned harmonics on Syndon Beta V, reduced by half the pleasures of a pitiable slug thing in the methane caves of Kkklll IV, enshrouded in bitterness and misery a man named Colin Marshack on an insignificant planet called Sol III, Earth, Terra, the world ...

And then, finally: I *will* know. I will *know!*

Trente removed the scale model of Earth from the display crate, and stared at it. Such a tiny thing, such a helpless thing, to support the nightwalk of a Paingod.

He selected the most recent recipient of his attentions, since one was as good as another; and using the means of travel his race had long since perfected, he left his encased cubicle hanging translucent against the stars. Trente, Paingod of the universes, for the first time in all the centuries he had lived that life of giving, never receiving, left his place, and left his Now, and went to find out. To find out ... what? He had no way of knowing.

For the Paingod, it was the first nightwalk.

Pieter Koslek had been born in a dwarf province of a miniscule Central European country long since swallowed up by a tiny power now a member of the Common Market. He had left Europe early in the 1920s, had shipped aboard a freighter to Bolivia, and after working his way as common deckhand

and laborer through half a dozen banana republics, had been washed up on an inland shore of the United States in 1934. He had promptly gone to earth, gone to seed, and gone to fat. A short stint in a CCC camp, a shorter stint as a bouncer in a Kansas City speak, a term in the Illinois State Workhouse, a long run on the Pontiac assembly line making an obscure part for an obscure segment of a B-17's innards, a brief fling as owner of a raspberry farm, and an extended period as a skid row—frequenting wino summed up his life. Now, as *now* would be reckoned by any sane man's table, Pieter Koslek was a wet brain—an alcoholic so sunk in the fumes and vapors of his own liquor need that he was barely recognizable as a human being. Lying soddenly, but quietly, in an alley two blocks up from the Greyhound bus station in downtown Los Angeles, Pieter Koslek, age 50, weight 210, hair filth grey, eyes red and moist and closed, unceremoniously died. That simply, that unconcernedly, that uneventfully for all the young-old men in overlong GI surplus overcoats who passed by that alley mouth unseeing, uncaring—Pieter Koslek died. His brain gave out, his lungs ceased to bellow, his heart refused to pump, his blood slid to a halt in his veins, and the breath no longer passed his lips. He died. End of story, beginning of story.

As he lay there, half-propped against the brick wall with its shredded reminder of a lightweight boxing match between two stumblebums long since passed into obscurity and the files of *Boxing Magazine*, a thin tepid vapor of pale green came to the body of Pieter Koslek; touched it; felt of it; entered it; Trente was on the planet Earth, Sol III.

If it had been possible to mount an epitaph on bronze for the wet brain, there on the wall of the alley perhaps, the most fitting would have been: HERE LAY PIETER KOSLEK. NOTHING IN HIS LIFE BECAME HIM SO MUCH AS THE LEAVING OF IT.

The thick-bodied orator on the empty packing crate had gathered a sizable crowd. His license was encased in plastic, and it had been pinned to a broom handle sharpened and driven into the ground. An American flag hung limply from a pole on the other side of the makeshift podium. The flag had only forty-eight stars; it had been purchased long before Hawaii or Alaska had joined the union, but new flags cost money, and—

"Scum! Like sewer water poured into your bloodstream! Look at them, do they *look* like you, do they *smell* like you—those smells, those, those *stinks* that walk like men! That's what they are, *stinks* with voting privileges, all of them, the niggers, the kike-Jews who own the land and the apartments you live in, what they think they're big deals! The spicks, the Puerto Rican filth that takes over your streets and rapes your women and puts its lousy hands on your white young daughters, that scum ..."

19

Colin Marshack stood in the crowd, staring up at the thick-bodied orator, his shaking hands thrust deep into his sport jacket pockets, his head throbbing, the unlit cigarette hanging unnoticed from his lips. Every word.

"... Commies in public office, is what we have got to be content with. Nigger lovers and pawns of the kike bastards who own the corporations. They wanta kill all of you, all of us, every one of us. They want us to say, 'Hey! C'mon, make love to my sister, to my wife, do all the dirty things that'll pollute my pure race!' That's what the Commies in public office, misusing *our* public trust, say to us. And what do we say in return, back to them, we say, 'No dice, dirty spicks, lousy kikes, Puerto bastards, black men that want to steal our pure heritage!' We say, go to hell to them, go straight to hell, you dirty rotten sonsuh—"

At which point the policemen moved quietly through the crowd, fascinated and silent like cobras at a mongoose convention, and arrested the thick-bodied orator.

As they took him away, Colin Marshack turned and moved out of the milling group. Why is such hideousness allowed to exist, he thought bitterly, fearfully. He walked down the path and out of Pershing Square ("Pershing Square is where they have a fence up so the fruits can't pick the people") and did not even realize the rheumy-eyed old man was following him till he was six blocks away.

Then he turned, and the old man almost ran into him. "Something I can do for you?" Colin Marshack asked.

The old man grinned feebly, his pale gums exposing themselves above gap-toothed ruin. "Nosir, nuh-nosir, Ise just, uh, I was uh just follerin' along to see maybe I could tap yuh for a coupla cents tuh get some chic'n noodle soup. It's kinda cold ... 'n I thought, maybe ..."

Colin Marshack's wide, somehow humorous face settled into understanding lines. "You're right, old man, it's cold, and it's windy, and it's miserable, and I think you're entitled to some goddam chicken noodle soup. God knows *someone's* entitled." He paused a moment, added, "Maybe me."

He took the old man by the arm, seemingly unaware of the rancid, rotting condition of the cloth. They walked along the street outside the park, and turned into one of the many side routes littered with one-arm beaneries and forty-cent-a-night flophouses.

"And possibly a hot roast beef sandwich with gravy all over the French fries," Colin added, steering the wine-smelling old derelict into a restaurant.

Over coffee and a bear claw, Colin Marshack stared at the old man. "Hey, what's your name?"

"Pieter Koslek," the old man murmured, hot vapors from the thick white coffee mug rising up before his watery eyes. "I've, uh, been kinda sick, y'know ..."

"Too much sauce, old man," said Colin Marshack. "Too much sauce does it for a lot of us. My father and mother both. Nice folk, loved each other, they went to the old alky's home hand-in-hand. It was touching."

"You're kinda feelin' sorry for y'self, ain'tcha?" noted Pieter Koslek and looked down at his coffee hurriedly.

Colin stared across angrily. Had he sunk that low, that even the seediest cockroach-ridden bum in the gutter could snipe at him, talk up to him, see his sad and sorry state? He tried to lift the coffee cup, and the cream-laced liquid sloshed over the rim, over his wrist. He yipped and set the cup down quickly.

"Your hands shake worse'n mine, mister," Pieter Koslek noted. It was a curious tone, somehow devoid of feeling or concern—more a statement of observation.

"Yeah, my hands shake, Mr. Koslek, sir. They shake because I make my living cutting things out of stone, and for the past two years I've been unable to get anything from stone but tidy piles of rock-dust."

Koslek spoke around a mouthful of cruller. "You uh you're one'a them statue makers, what I mean a sculpt'r."

"That is precisely what I am, Mr. Koslek, sir. I am a capturer of exquisite beauty in rock and plaster and quartz and marble. The only trouble is, I'm no damned good, and I was never *ever* really very good, but at least I made a decent living selling a piece here and there, and conning myself into thinking I was great and building a career, and even Canaday in the *Times* said a few nice things about me. But even *that's* turned to rust now. I can't make a chisel do what I want it to do, I can't sand and I can't chip and I can't carve dirty words on sidewalks if I try."

Pieter Koslek stared across at Colin Marshack, and there was a banked fire down in those rheumy, sad old eyes. He watched and looked and saw the hands shaking uncontrollably, saw them wring one against another like mad things, and even when interlocked, they still trembled hideously.

And ...

Trente, locked within an alien shell, comprehended a small something. This creature of puny carbon atoms and other substances that could not exist for an instant in the rigorous arena of space, was dying. Inside, it was ending its life-cycle, because of the misery Trente had sent down. Trente had been responsible for the quivering pain that sent Colin Marshack's hands into spasms. It had been done two years before—by Colin Marshack's time—but only a few moments earlier as Trente knew it. And now it had changed this creature's life totally. Trente watched the strange human being, a product of little introverted needs and desires, here on this mudball circling a nothing star in a far outpost of nowhere. And he knew he must go further, must experiment further with his problem. The green and transparent vapor that was Trente seeped out of the eyes of Pieter Koslek, and slid carefully inside Colin Marshack. It left itself wide open, flung itself wide open, to what tremors governed the man. And Trente felt the full

21

impact of the pain he so lightly dispensed to all the living things in the universes. It was potent hot all! And it was a further knowing, a greater knowledge, a simple act that the sickness had compelled him to undertake. By the fear and the memory of all the fears that had gone before, Trente knew, *and knowing, had to go further. For he was Paingod, not a transient tourist in the country of pain. He drew forth the mind of Marshack, of that weak and trembling Colin Marshack, and fled with it. Out. Out there. Further. Much further. Till time came to a slithering halt and space was no longer of any consequence. And he whirled Colin Marshack through the universes. Through the infinite allness of the space and time and motion and meaning that was the crevice into which Life had sunk itself. He saw the blobs of mud and the whirling winged things and the tall humanoids and the cleat-treaded half-men/half-machines that ruled one and another sector of open space. He showed it all to Colin Marshack, drenched him in wonder, filled him like the most vital goblet the Ethos had ever created, poured him full of love and life and the staggering beauty of the cosmos. And having done that, he whirled the soul and spirit of Colin Marshack down, down, and down to the fibrous shell that was his body, and poured that soul back inside. Then he walked the shell to the home of Colin Marshack ... and turned it loose. And ...*

When the sculptor awoke, lying face down amidst the marble chips and powder-fine dust of the statue, he saw the base first; and not having recalled even buying a chunk of stone that large, raised himself on his hands, and his knees, and his haunches, and sat there, and his eyes went up toward the summit, and seemed to go on forever, and when he finally saw what it was he had created—this thing of such incredible loveliness and meaning and wisdom— he began to sob. Softly, never very loud, but deeply, as though each whimper was drawn from the very core of him.

He had done it this once, but as he saw his hands still trembling, still murmuring to themselves in spasm, he knew it was the one time he would ever do it. There was no memory of how, or why, or even of when ... but it was *his* work, of that he was certain. The pains in his wrists told him it was.

The moment of truth stood high above him, resplendent in marble and truth, but there would be no other moments.

This was Colin Marshack's life, in its totality, now.

The sound of sobbing was only broken periodically, as he began to drink.

Waiting. The Ethos waited. Trente had known they would be. It was inevitable. Foolish for him to conceive of a situation in which they would not have an awareness.

Away. From your post, away.

"I had to know. It has been growing in me, a live thing in me. I had to know. It was the only way. I went to a planet, and lived within what they call 'men' and knew. I think I understand now."

Know. What is it you know?

"I know that pain is the most important thing in the universes. Greater than survival, greater than love, greater even than the beauty it brings about. For without pain there can be no pleasure. Without sadness there can be no happiness. Without misery there can be no beauty. And without these, life is endless, hopeless, doomed, and damned."

Adult. You have become adult.

"I know ... this is what became of the other Paingods before me. They grew into concern, into knowing, and then ..."

Lost. They were lost to us.

"They could not take the step; they could not go to one of the ones to whom they had sent pain, and learn. So they were no use as Paingods. I understood. Now I know, and I am returned."

Do. What will you do?

"I will send more pain than ever before. More and greater."

More? You will send more?

"Much more. And again, more. Because now I understand. It is a grey and a lonely place in which we live, all of us, swinging between desperation and emptiness, and all that makes it worthwhile is caring, is beauty. But if there was no opposite for beauty, if there was no opposite for pleasure, it would all turn to dust, to waste."

Being. Now you know who you are.

"I am most blessed of the Ethos, and most humble. You have given me the highest, kindest position in the universes. For I am the God to all men, and to all creatures small and large, whether they call me by name or not. I am Paingod, and it is my life, however long it stretches, to treat them to the finest they will ever know. To give them pain, that they may know pleasure. Thank you."

And the Ethos went away, secure that at last, after all the eons of Paingods who had broken under the strain, who had lacked the courage to take that nightwalk, they had found one who would last truly forever. Trente had come of age.

While back in the cubicle, hanging star-bright and translucent in space, high above it all, yet very much part of it all, the creature who would never die; the creature who had lived within the rotting body of Pieter Koslek and for a few moments in the soul and talent of Colin Marshack, that creature called Paingod, learned one more thing, as he stared at the tiny model of the planet Earth he had known.

Trente knew the feel of a tear formed in a duct and turned free from an eye globe—cool on his face.

Trente knew happiness.

23

Now it can be told: my secret vice. Buried deep in the anthracite core of my being is a personal trait so hideous, so confounding, a conceit so terrible in its repercussions, that it makes sodomy, pederasty, and barratry on the high seas seem as tame as a Frances Parkinson Keyes novel. I am always late. Invariably. Consistently. If I tell you I'll be there to pick up you at 8:30, expect me Thursday. A positive genius for tardiness. Paramount sends a car to pick me up when I'm scripting, otherwise they know I'll be off looking at the flowers, or watching the ocean, or reading a copy of The Amazing Spider-Man *in the bathroom. I have been brought to task for this, on innumerable occasions. It prompted several courts-martial when I was in the Army. I've lost girlfriends because of it. So I went to a doctor, to see if there was something wrong with my medulla oblongata, or somesuch. He told me I was always late. His bill was seventy-five dollars. I've decided that unlike most other folk with highly developed senses of the fluidity of time, the permanence of humanity in the chrono-stream, et al, I got no ticktock going up there on top. So I had to explain it to the world, to cop out, as it were, in advance. I wrote the following story as my plea for understanding, extrapolating the (to me) ghastly state of the world around me—in which everyone scampers here and there to be places on time—to a time not too far away (by my watch) in which you get your life docked every time you're late. It is not entirely coincidental that the name of the hero in this minor masterpiece closely resembles that of the author, to wit:*

25

"Repent, Harlequin!"
Said the Ticktockman

There are always those who ask, what is it all about? For those who need to ask, for those who need points sharply made, who need to know "where it's at," this:

"The mass of men serve the state thus, not as men mainly, but as machines, with their bodies. They are the standing army, and the militia, jailors, constables, posse comitatus, etc. In most cases there is no free exercise whatever of the judgment or of the moral sense; but they put themselves on a level with wood and earth and stones; and wooden men can perhaps be manufactured that will serve the purpose as well. Such command no more respect than men of straw or a lump of dirt. They have the same sort of worth only as horses and dogs. Yet such as these even are commonly esteemed good citizens. Others—as most legislators, politicians, lawyers, ministers, and officeholders— serve the state chiefly with their heads; and, as they rarely make any moral distinctions, they are as likely to serve the Devil, without intending it, as God. A very few, as heroes, patriots, martyrs, reformers in the great sense, and men, serve the state with their consciences also, and so necessarily resist it for the most part; and they are commonly treated as enemies by it."

Henry David Thoreau,
CIVIL DISOBEDIENCE

That is the heart of it. Now begin in the middle, and later learn the beginning; the end will take care of itself.

But because it was the very world it was, the very world they had allowed
it to *become*, for months his activities did not come to the alarmed attention of
The Ones Who Kept the Machine Functioning Smoothly, the ones who
poured the very best butter over the cams and mainsprings of the culture. Not
until it had become obvious that somehow, someway, he had become a noto-
riety, a celebrity, perhaps even a hero for (what Officialdom inescapably
tagged) "an emotionally disturbed segment of the populace," did they turn it
over to the Ticktockman and his legal machinery. But by then, because it was
the very world it was, and they had no way to predict he would happen—possibly a strain of disease long-defunct, now, suddenly, reborn in a system where
immunity had been forgotten, had lapsed—he had been allowed to become
too real. Now he had form and substance.

He had become a *personality*, something they had filtered out of the system
many decades before. But there it was, and there *he* was, a very definitely
imposing personality. In certain circles—middle-class circles—it was thought
disgusting. Vulgar ostentation. Anarchistic. Shameful. In others, there was
only sniggering: those strata where thought is subjugated to form and ritual,
niceties, proprieties. But down below, ah, down below, where the people
always needed their saints and sinners, their bread and circuses, their heroes
and villains, he was considered a Bolivar; a Napoleon; a Robin Hood; a Dick
Bong (Ace of Aces); a Jesus; a Jomo Kenyatta.

And at the top—where, like socially-attuned Shipwreck Kellys, every
tremor and vibration threatens to dislodge the wealthy, powerful, and tilted from their flagpoles—he was considered a menace; a heretic; a rebel; a
disgrace; a peril. He was known down the line, to the very heart-meat core,
but the important reactions were high above and far below. At the very
top, at the very bottom.

So his file was turned over, along with his time-card and his cardioplate,
to the office of Ticktockman.

The Ticktockman: very much over six feet tall, often silent, a soft purring
man when things went timewise. The Ticktockman.

Even in the cubicles of the hierarchy, where fear was generated, seldom suffered, he was called the Ticktockman. But no one called him that
to his mask.

You don't call a man a hated name, not when that man, behind his mask,
is capable of revoking the minutes, the hours, the days and nights, the
years of your life. He was called the Master Timekeeper to his mask. It was
safer that way.

27

"This is *what* he is," said the Ticktockman with genuine softness, "but not *who* he is. This time-card I'm holding in my left hand has a name on it, but it is the name of *what* he is, not *who* he is. The cardioplate here in my right hand is also named, but not *whom* named, merely *what* named. Before I can exercise proper revocation, I have to know *who* this *what* is."

To his staff, all the ferrets, all the loggers, all the finks, all the commex, even the mineez, he said, "Who is this Harlequin?"

He was not purring smoothly. Timewise, it was jangle.

However, it *was* the longest speech they had ever heard him utter at one time, the staff, the ferrets, the loggers, the finks, the commex, but not the mineez, who usually weren't around to know, in any case. But even they scurried to find out.

Who is the Harlequin?

High above the third level of the city, he crouched on the humming aluminum-frame platform of the air-boat (foof! air-boat, indeed! swizzleskid is what it was, with a tow-rack jerry-rigged) and he stared down at the neat Mondrian arrangement of the buildings.

Somewhere nearby, he could hear the metronomic left-right-left of the 2:47 P.M. shift, entering the Timkin roller-bearing plant in their sneakers. A minute later, precisely, he heard the softer right-left-right of the 5:00 A.M. formation, going home.

An elfin grin spread across his tanned features, and his dimples appeared for a moment. Then, scratching at his thatch of auburn hair, he shrugged within his motley, as though girding himself for what came next, and threw the joystick forward, and bent into the wind as the airboat dropped. He skimmed over a slidewalk, purposely dropping a few feet to crease the tassels of the ladies of fashion, and—inserting thumbs in large ears—he stuck out his tongue, rolled his eyes and went wugga-wugga-wugga. It was a minor diversion. One pedestrian skittered and tumbled, sending parcels everywhichway, another wet herself, a third keeled slantwise, and the walk was stopped automatically by the servitors till she could be resuscitated. It was a minor diversion.

Then he swirled away on a vagrant breeze, and was gone. Hi-ho.

As he rounded the cornice of the Time-Motion Study Building, he saw the shift, just boarding the slidewalk. With practiced motion and an absolute conservation of movement, they side-stepped up onto the slow-strip and (in a chorus line reminiscent of a Busby Berkeley film of the antediluvian 1930s) advanced across the strips ostrich-walking till they were lined upon the expresstrip.

Once more, in anticipation, the elfin grin spread, and there was a tooth missing back there on the left side. He dipped, skimmed, and swooped over them; and then, scrunching about on the air-boat, he released the holding pins that fastened shut the ends of the homemade pouring troughs that kept his cargo from dumping prematurely. And as he pulled the trough-pins, the air-boat slid over the factory workers and one hundred and fifty thousand dollars worth of jelly beans cascaded down on the expresstrip.

Jelly beans! Millions and billions of purples and yellows and greens and licorice and grape and raspberry and mint and round and smooth and crunchy outside and soft-mealy inside and sugary and bouncing jouncing tumbling clittering clattering skittering fell on the heads and shoulders and hardhats and carapaces of the Timkin workers, tinkling on the slidewalk and bouncing away and rolling about underfoot and filling the sky on their way down with all the colors of joy and childhood and holidays, coming down in a steady rain, a solid wash, a torrent of color and sweetness out of the sky from above, and entering a universe of sanity and metronomic order with quite-mad coocoo newness. Jelly beans!

The shift workers howled and laughed and were pelted, and broke ranks, and the jelly beans managed to work their way into the mechanism of the slidewalks after which there was a hideous scraping as the sound of a million fingernails rasped down a quarter of a million blackboards, followed by a coughing and a sputtering, and then the slidewalks all stopped and everyone was dumped thisawayandthataway in a jackstraw tumble, still laughing and popping little jelly bean eggs of childish color into their mouths. It was a holiday, and a jollity, an absolute insanity, a giggle. But ...

The shift was delayed seven minutes.

They did not get home for seven minutes.

The master schedule was thrown off by seven minutes.

Quotas were delayed by inoperative slidewalks for seven minutes.

He had tapped the first domino in the line, and one after another, like chik chik chik, the others had fallen.

The System had been seven minutes worth of disrupted. It was a tiny matter, one hardly worthy of note, but in a society where the single driving force was order and unity and equality and promptness and clocklike precision and attention to the clock, reverence of the gods of the passage of time, it was a disaster of major importance.

So he was ordered to appear before the Ticktockman. It was broadcast across every channel of the communications web. He was ordered to be *there* at 7:00 dammit on time. And they waited, and they waited, but he didn't show up till almost ten-thirty, at which time he merely sang a little song about moonlight in a place no one had ever heard of, called Vermont, and vanished again. But they had all been waiting since seven, and it wrecked *hell* with their schedules. So the question remained: Who is the Harlequin?

29

But the *unasked* question (more important of the two) was: how did we get *into* this position, where a laughing, irresponsible japer of jabberwocky and jive could disrupt our entire economic and cultural life with a hundred and fifty thousand dollars worth of jelly beans ...

Jelly for God's sake *beans!* This is madness! Where did he get the money to buy a hundred and fifty thousand dollars worth of jelly beans? (They knew it would have cost that much, because they had a team of Situation Analysts pulled off another assignment and rushed to the slidewalk scene to sweep up and count the candies, and produce findings, which disrupted *their* schedules and threw their entire branch at least a day behind.) Jelly beans! Jelly ... *beans?* Now wait a second—a second accounted for—no one has manufactured jelly beans for over a hundred years. Where did he get jelly beans?

That's another good question. More than likely it will never be answered to your complete satisfaction. But then, how many questions ever are?

The middle you know. Here is the beginning. How it starts:

A desk pad. Day for day, and turn each day. 9:00—open the mail. 9:45— appointment with planning commission board. 10:30—discuss installation progress charts with J.L. 11:45—pray for rain. 12:00—lunch. *And so it goes.*

"I'm sorry, Miss Grant, but the time for interviews was set at 2:30, and it's almost five now. I'm sorry you're late, but those are the rules. You'll have to wait till next year to submit application for this college again." *And so it goes.*

The 10:10 local stops at Cresthaven, Galesville, Tonawanda Junction, Selby, and Farnhurst, but not at Indiana City, Lucasville, and Colton, except on Sunday. The 10:35 express stops at Galesville, Selby, and Indiana City, except on Sundays & Holidays, at which time it stops at ... *and so it goes.*

"I couldn't wait, Fred. I had to be at Pierre Cartain's by 3:00, and you said you'd meet me under the clock in the terminal at 2:45, and you weren't there, so I had to go on. You're always late, Fred. If you'd been there, we could have sewed it up together, but as it was, well, I took the order alone ..." *And so it goes.*

Dear Mr. and Mrs. Atterley: in reference to your son Gerold's constant tardiness, I am afraid we will have to suspend him from school unless some more reliable method can be instituted guaranteeing he will arrive at his classes on time. Granted he is an exemplary student, and his marks are high, his constant flouting of the schedules of this school makes it impractical to maintain him in a system where the other children seem capable of getting where they are supposed to be on time *and so it goes.*

YOU CANNOT VOTE UNLESS YOU APPEAR AT 8:45 A.M.

"I don't care if the script is *good*, I need it Thursday!"

CHECK-OUT TIME IS 2:00 P.M.

"You got here late. The job's taken. Sorry."

YOUR SALARY HAS BEEN DOCKED FOR TWENTY MINUTES TIME LOST.

"God, what time is it, I've gotta run!"

And so it goes. And so it goes. And so it goes. And so it goes goes goes goes goes tick tock tick tock tick tock and one day we no longer let time serve us, we serve time and we are slaves of the schedule, worshippers of the sun's passing; bound into a life predicated on restrictions because the system will not function if we don't keep the schedule tight.

Until it becomes more than a minor inconvenience to be late. It becomes a sin. Then a crime. Then a crime punishable by this:

EFFECTIVE 15 JULY 2389 12:00:00 midnight, the office of the Master Timekeeper will require all citizens to submit their time-cards and cardio-plates for processing. In accordance with Statute 555-7-SGH-999 governing the revocation of time per capita, all cardioplates will be keyed to the individual holder and—

What they had done, was to devise a method of curtailing the amount of life a person could have. If he was ten minutes late, he lost ten minutes of his life. An hour was proportionately worth more revocation. If someone was consistently tardy, he might find himself, on a Sunday night, receiving a communiqué from the Master Timekeeper that his time had run out, and he would be "turned off" at high noon on Monday, please straighten your affairs, sir, madame, or bisex.

And so, by this simple scientific expedient (utilizing a scientific process held dearly secret by the Ticktockman's office) the System was maintained. It was the only expedient thing to do. It was, after all, patriotic. The schedules had to be met. After all, there *was* a war on!

But wasn't there always?

"Now that is really disgusting," the Harlequin said, when Pretty Alice showed him the wanted poster. "Disgusting and *highly* improbable. After all, this isn't the days of desperadoes. A *wanted* poster!"

"You know," Pretty Alice noted, "you speak with a great deal of inflection."

"I'm sorry," said the Harlequin, humbly.

"No need to be sorry. You're always saying 'I'm sorry.' You have such massive guilt, Everett, it's really very sad."

"I'm sorry," he repeated, then pursed his lips so the dimples appeared momentarily. He hadn't wanted to say that at all. "I have to go out again. I have to *do* something."

Pretty Alice slammed her coffee-bulb down on the counter. "Oh for God's *sake*, Everett, can't you stay home just *one* night! Must you always be out in that ghastly clown suit, running around annoying people?"

31

"I'm—" He stopped, and clapped the jester's hat onto his auburn thatch with a tiny tingling of bells. He rose, rinsed out his coffee-bulb at the spray, and put it into the drier for a moment. "I have to go."

She didn't answer. The faxbox was purring, and she pulled a sheet out, read it, threw it toward him on the counter. "It's about you. Of course. You're ridiculous."

He read it quickly. It said the Ticktockman was trying to locate him. He didn't care, he was going out to be late again. At the door, dredging for an exit line, he hurled back petulantly, "Well, *you* speak with inflection, *too!*"

Pretty Alice rolled her pretty eyes heavenward. "You're ridiculous." The Harlequin stalked out, slamming the door, which sighed shut softly, and locked itself.

There was a gentle knock, and Pretty Alice got up with an exhalation of exasperated breath, and opened the door. He stood there. "I'll be back about ten-thirty, okay?"

She pulled a rueful face. "Why do you tell me that? Why? You *know* you'll be late! You *know it!* You're *always* late, so why do you tell me these dumb things?" She closed the door.

On the other side, the Harlequin nodded to himself. *She's right. She's always right. I'll be late. I'm always late. Why do I tell her these dumb things?*

He shrugged again, and went off to be late once more.

He had fired off the firecracker rockets that said: I will attend the 115th annual International Medical Association Invocation at 8:00 P.M. precisely. I do hope you will all be able to join me.

The words had burned in the sky, and of course the authorities were there, lying in wait for him. They assumed, naturally, that he would be late. He arrived twenty minutes early, while they were setting up the spiderwebs to trap and hold him. Blowing a large bullhorn, he frightened and unnerved them so, their own moisturized encirclement webs sucked closed, and they were hauled up, kicking and shrieking, high above the amphitheater's floor. The Harlequin laughed and laughed, and apologized profusely. The physicians, gathered in solemn conclave, roared with laughter, and accepted the Harlequin's apologies with exaggerated bowing and posturing, and a merry time was had by all, who thought the Harlequin was a regular foofaraw in fancy pants; all, that is, but the authorities, who had been sent out by the office of the Ticktockman; they hung there like so much dockside cargo, hauled up above the floor of the amphitheater in a most unseemly fashion.

(In another part of the same city where the Harlequin carried on his "activities," totally unrelated in every way to what concerns us here, save that it illustrates the Ticktockman's power and import, a man named Marshall

Delahanty received his turn-off notice from the Ticktockman's office. His wife received the notification from the gray-suited minee who delivered it, with the traditional "look of sorrow" plastered hideously across his face. She knew what it was, even without unsealing it. It was a billet-doux of immediate recognition to everyone these days. She gasped, and held it as though it were a glass slide tinged with botulism, and prayed it was not for her. Let it be for Marsh, she thought, brutally, realistically, or one of the kids, but not for me, please dear God, not for me. And then she opened it, and it *was* for Marsh, and she was at one and the same time horrified and relieved. The next trooper in the line had caught the bullet. "Marshall," she screamed, "Marshall! Termination, Marshall! Ohmigod, Marshall, whattl we do, whattl we do, Marshall omigod-marshall ..." and in their home that night was the sound of tearing paper and fear, and the stink of madness went up the flue and there was nothing, absolutely nothing they could do about it.

(But Marshall Delahanty tried to run. And early the next day, when turn-off time came, he was deep in the Canadian forest two hundred miles away, and the office of the Ticktockman blanked his cardioplate, and Marshall Delahanty keeled over, running, and his heart stopped, and the blood dried up on its way to his brain, and he was dead, that's all. One light went out on the sector map in the office of the Master Timekeeper, while notification was entered for fax reproduction, and Georgette Delahanty's name was entered on the dole roles till she could remarry. Which is the end of the footnote, and all the point that need be made, except don't laugh, because that is what would happen to the Harlequin if ever the Ticktockman found out his real name. It isn't funny.)

The shopping level of the city was thronged with the Thursday-colors of the buyers. Women in canary yellow chitons and men in pseudo-Tyrolean outfits that were jade and leather and fit very tightly, save for the balloon pants.

When the Harlequin appeared on the still-being-constructed shell of the new Efficiency Shopping Center, his bullhorn to his elfishly-laughing lips, everyone pointed and stared, and he berated them:

"Why let them order you about? Why let them tell you to hurry and scurry like ants or maggots? Take your time! Saunter a while! Enjoy the sunshine, enjoy the breeze, let life carry you at your own pace! Don't be slaves of time, it's a helluva way to die, slowly, by degrees ... down with the Ticktockman!"

Who's the nut? Most of the shoppers wanted to know. Who's the nut oh wow I'm gonna be late I gotta run ... .

And the construction gang on the Shopping Center received an urgent order from the office of the Master Timekeeper that the dangerous criminal known as the Harlequin was atop their spire, and their aid was urgently needed in apprehending him. The work crew said no, they would lose time on their construction schedule, but the Ticktockman managed to pull the proper threads of governmental webbing, and they were told to cease work and catch that nitwit up there on the spire; up there with the bullhorn. So a dozen and more burly workers began climbing into their construction platforms, releasing the a-gray plates, and rising toward the Harlequin.

After the debacle (in which, through the Harlequin's attention to personal safety, no one was seriously injured), the workers tried to reassemble, and assault him again, but it was too late. He had vanished. It had attracted quite a crowd, however, and the shopping cycle was thrown off by hours, simply hours. The purchasing needs of the system were therefore falling behind, and so measures were taken to accelerate the cycle for the rest of the day, but it got bogged down and speeded up and they sold too many float-valves and not nearly enough wegglers, which meant that the popli ratio was off, which made it necessary to rush cases and cases of spoiling Smash-O to stores that usually needed a case only every three or four hours. The shipments were bollixed, the transshipments were misrouted and, in the end, even the swizzleskid industries felt it.

"Don't come back till you have him!" the Ticktockman said, very quietly, very sincerely, extremely dangerously.

They used dogs. They used probes. They used cardioplate cross-offs. They used teepers. They used bribery. They used stiktytes. They used intimidation. They used torment. They used torture. They used finks. They used cops. They used search&seizure. They used fallaron. They used betterment incentive. They used fingerprints. They used the Bertillon system. They used cunning. They used guile. They used treachery. They used Raoul Mitgong, but he didn't help much. They used applied physics. They used techniques of criminology.

And what the hell: they caught him.

After all, his name was Everett C. Marm, and he wasn't much to begin with, except a man who had no sense of time.

"Repent, Harlequin!" said the Ticktockman.

"Get stuffed!" the Harlequin replied, sneering.

"You've been late a total of sixty-three years, five months, three weeks, two days, twelve hours, forty-one minutes, fifty-nine seconds, point oh three six one one one microseconds. You've used up everything you can, and more. I'm going to turn you off."

"Scare someone else. I'd rather be dead than live in a dumb world with a bogeyman like you."

"It's my job."

"You're full of it. You're a tyrant. You have no right to order people around and kill them if they show up late."

34

"You can't adjust. You can't fit in."

"Unstrap me, and I'll fit my fist into your mouth."

"You're a nonconformist."

"That didn't used to be a felony."

"It is now. Live in the world around you."

"I hate it. It's a terrible world."

"Not everyone thinks so. Most people enjoy order."

"I don't, and most of the people I know don't."

"That's not true. How do you think we caught you?"

"I'm not interested."

"A girl named Pretty Alice told us who you were."

"That's a lie."

"It's true. You unnerve her. She wants to belong, she wants to conform, I'm going to turn you off."

"Then do it already, and stop arguing with me."

"I'm not going to turn you off."

"You're an idiot!"

"Repent, Harlequin!" said the Ticktockman.

"Get stuffed."

So they sent him to Coventry. And in Coventry they worked him over. It was just like what they did to Winston Smith in *1984*, which was a book none of them knew about, but the techniques are really quite ancient, and so they did it to Everett C. Marm, and one day quite a long time later, the Harlequin appeared on the communications web, appearing elfin and dimpled and bright-eyed, and not at all brainwashed, and he said he had been wrong, that it was a good, a very good thing indeed, to belong, to be right on time hip-ho and away we go, and everyone stared up at him on the public screens that covered an entire city block, and they said to themselves, well, you see, he was just a nut after all, and if that's the way the system is run, then let's do it that way, because it doesn't pay to fight city hall, or in this case, the Ticktockman. So Everett C. Marm was destroyed, which was a loss, because of what Thoreau said earlier, but you can't make an omelet without breaking a few eggs, and in every revolution a few die who shouldn't, but they have to, because that's the way it happens, and if you make only a little change, then it seems to be worthwhile. Or, to make the point lucidly:

"Uh, excuse me, sir, I, uh, don't know how to uh, to uh, tell you this, but you were three minutes late. The schedule is a little, uh, bit off."

He grinned sheepishly.

"That's ridiculous!" murmured the Ticktockman behind his mask. "Check your watch." And then he went into his office, going mrmee, mrmee, mrmee, mrmee.

Madness is in the eye of the beholder.

Having done exhaustive research on sociopathic behavior for a two-hour NBC dramatic special recently, I won't give you the faintest murmur of an objection that there are freaks and whackos walking the streets; they're as liable to shoot you dead for chuckles as they are to assist you in getting your stalled car moving out of the intersection. One reliable estimate of the number of potential psychomotor epileptics undetected in our midst is 250,000 in the United States alone. And if you've read Michael Crichton's TERMINAL MAN you know that the "brain storm" caused by psychomotor epilepsy can turn a normal human being into a psychopathic killer in moments. No, I won't argue: there are madfolk among us.

But the madness of which I speak is what the late George Apley might have called "eccentricity." The behavioral pattern outside the accepted norm. Whatever the hell that might be. The little old man sitting on the park bench having an animated conversation with himself. The girl who likes to dress as an exact replica of Betty Boop. The young guy out on the sidewalk playing an ocarina and interspersing his recital with denunciations of the city power and water authority. The old lady who dies in her two-room flat and the cops find sixty years' worth of old newspapers plus two hundred thousand dollars in a cigar box. (One of the wooden ones, the old ones you simply can't find any more because they don't make them. They're great for storing old photos and comic character buttons. If you have one you don't want, send it along to me, willya?) The staid businessman who gets off by wearing his wife's pantyhose. The little kid who puts a big "S" on a bath towel and, shouting, "Up, up and awaaayyy!" jumps off the garage roof.

They're not nuts, friends, they're simply seeing it all through different eyes. They have imagination, and they know something about being alone and in pain. They're altering the real world to fit their fantasies. That's okay.

We all do it. Don't say you don't. How many of you have come out of the movie, having seen Bullitt or The French Connection or Vanishing Point or The Last American Hero or Freebie and the Bean, gotten in your car, and just about done a wheelie, sixty-five mph out of the parking lot? Don't lie to me, gentle reader, we all have weird-looking mannerisms that seem perfectly rational to us, but make onlookers cock an eyebrow and cross to the other side of the street.

I've grown very fond of people who can let it out, who can have the strength of compulsion to indulge their special affectations. They seem to me more real than the faceless gray hordes of sidewalk sliders who go from there to here without so much as a hop, skip, or a jump.

One morning in New York last year, I was having a drug-store breakfast with Nancy Weber, who wrote THE LIFE SWAP. We were sitting up at the counter, on revolving stools, chewing down greasy eggs and salty bacon, talking about how many dryads can live in a banyan tree, when the front door of the drug store (the now-razed, much-lamented, lovely Henry Halper's on the corner of 56th and Madison, torn down to build, I suppose, an aesthetically-enchanting parking structure or candidate for a towering inferno) opened, and in stormed a little old man in an overcoat much too heavy for the weather. He boiled in like a monsoon, stood in the middle of the room and began to pillory Nixon and his resident offensive line of thugs for double-teaming Democracy. He was brilliant. Never repeated himself once. And this was long before the crash of Nixon off his pedestal. Top of his lungs. Flamboyant rhetoric. Utter honesty, no mickeymouse, corruption and evil a-flower in the land of the free! On and on he went, as everyone stared dumbfounded. And then, without even a bow to the box seats, out he went, a breath of fresh air in a muggy world. I sat there with a grin on my face only a tape measure could have recorded. I applauded. Superduper! Nancy dug it, I dug it, and a bespectacled gentleman three down from us—burnt toast ignored—dug it. The rest of the people vacillated between outrage and confusion, finally settling on attitudes best described by a circling finger toward the right ear. They thought he was bananas. Well, maybe, but what a swell madness!

Or take my bed, for instance.

When you come into my bedroom, you see the bed up on a square box platform covered with deep pile carpeting. It's in bright colors, because I like bright colors. Now, there's a very good, solid, rational reason why the bed is up there like that. Some day I'll tell you why; it's a personal reason; in the nature of killing evil shadows. But that isn't important, right here. What is important is the attitude of people who see that bed for the first time. Some snicker and call it an altar. Others frown in disapproval and call it a pedestal, or a

Playboy *bed. It's none of those. It's very functional, and serves an emotional purpose that is none of their business, but Lord, how quick they are to label it the way they see it, and to lay **their** value judgment on it and me. Most of the time I don't bother explaining. It isn't worth it.*

But it happens all the time, and every time it happens I think about this story. Madness is in the eye of the beholder. What seems cuckoo to you may be rigorously logical to someone else. Remember that as you read.

The Crackpots

He was standing on a street corner, wearing a long orange night-gown and a red slumber-cap with a tassel. He was studiously picking his nose.

"Watch him!" cried Furth. "Watch what he does! Get the technique accurately!"

For this I studied four years to become an expert? thought Themus.

Furth looked at the younger man for the first time in several minutes. "Are you watching him?" The elder Watcher nudged his companion, causing Themus's dictobox to bump unceremoniously against his chest.

"Yes, yes, I'm watching," answered Themus, "but what possible reason could there be to watch a lunatic picking his nose on a public street corner?" Annoyance rang in his voice.

Furth swung on him, his eyes cold-steel. "You *watch* them, that's your job. And don't ever forget that! And dictate it into that box strapped to your stupid shoulders. If I ever catch you failing to notice and dictate what they're doing, I'll have you shipped back to Central and then into the Mines. You understand what I'm saying?"

Themus nodded dumbly, the attack having shocked and surprised him, so sudden and intensive was it.

He watched the Crackpot.

His stomach felt uneasy. His voice quavered as he described in minute detail, as he had been taught, the procedure. It made his nose itch. He ignored it. Soon the Crackpot gave a little laugh, did a small dance step, and skipped out of sight across the street and around the corner.

Themus spoke into the Communicator-Attachment on his box: "Watcher, sector seventy, here. Male, orange nightgown, red slumber-cap, coming your way. Pick him up, sixty-nine. He's all yours. Over."

An acknowledging buzz came from the Attachment. Themus said, "Out here," and turned the Attachment off.

Furth, who had been dictating the detailed tying of a can on the tail of a four-legged Kyben dog by a tall, bald Crackpot, concluded his report as the dog ran off barking wildly, muttered, "Off," into the dictobox and turned once more to Themus. The younger Watcher tightened inside. *Here it comes.*

Unexpectedly, the senior Watcher's voice was quiet, almost gentle. "Come with me, Themus, I want to talk with you."

They strode through the street of Valasah, capital of Kyba, watching the other branch of Kyben. The native Kyben, those who put light-tubes in their mouths and twisted their ears in expectation of fluorescence, those who pulled their teeth with adjusto-wrenches, those who sat and scribbled odd messages on the sidewalks, called the armor-dressed Kyben "Stuffed Shirts." The governing Kyben, those with the armor and high-crested metal helmets bearing the proud emblem of the eye-and-eagle, called their charges "Crackpots."

They were both Kyben.

There was a vast difference.

Furth was about to delineate the difference to his new aide. The senior Watcher's great cape swirled in a rain of black as he turned into the Pub crawler.

At a table near the front, Furth pulled his cape about his thighs and sat down, motioning Themus to the other chair.

The waiter walked slowly over to them, yawning behind his hand. Furth dictated the fact briefly. The waiter gave a high-pitched maniacal laugh. Themus felt his blood chill. These people were all mad, absolutely mad.

"Two glasses of *gretb*," Furth said.

The waiter left. Furth recorded the fact. The waiter had kicked him before he had gone behind the bar.

When the drinks arrived, Furth took a long pull from the helix-shaped glass, slumped back, folded his hands on the table and said, "What did you learn at Academy-Central?"

The question took Themus by surprise. "Wh-what do you mean? I learned a great many things."

41

"Such as? Tell me."

"Well, there was primary snooping, both conscious and subconscious evaluation, reportage—four full years of it—shorthand, applied dictology, history, manners, customs, authority evaluation, mechanics, fact assemblage ..."

He found the subjects leaping to the front of his mind, tumbling from his lips. He had been second in his class of twelve hundred, and it had all stuck.

Furth cut him off with a wave of his hand. "Let's take that history. Capsule it for me."

Furth was a big man, eyes oddly set far back in hollows above deep yellow cheeks, hair white about the temples, a lean and electric man, the type who radiates energy even when asleep. Themus suspected this was his superior's way of testing him. He recited:

"The Corps is dedicated to gathering data. It will Watch and detect, assimilate and file. Nothing will escape the gaze of the Watcher. As the eagle soars, so the eye of the Watcher will fly to all things."

"God, *no*, man, I mean the *History!* The *History.*" The elder Watcher precision-tapped his fingers one after another in irritation. "What is the story of the Kyben. Of Kyba itself. Of your job here. What is our relation to these?"

He waved his hand, taking in the bar, the people in the streets, the entire planet and its twin suns blazing yellow in the afternoon sky.

Themus licked his thin lips, "The Kyben rule the Galaxy—is that what you want?" He breathed easier as the older man nodded. He continued, by rote: "The Kyben rule the Galaxy. They are the organizers. All other races realize the superior reasoning and administrative powers of the Kyben, and thus allow the Kyben to rule the Galaxy."

He stopped, biting his lower lip, "With your permission, Superior, can I do this some other way? Back at Academy-Central memorization was required, even on Penares it seemed apropos, but somehow—*here*—it sounds foolish to me. No disrespect intended, you understand, I'd just like to ramble it off quickly. I gather all you want are the basics."

The older man nodded his head for Themus to continue in any fashion he chose.

"We are a power, and all the others are too scared of us to try usurping because we run it all better than any ten of them could, and the only trouble is with the Earthmen and the Mawson Confederation, with whom we are negotiating right now. The only thing we have against us is this planet of black-sheep relatives. They happen to be our people, but we left them some eleven hundred years ago because they were a pain in the neck and the Kyben realized they had a universe to conquer, and we wish we could get rid of them, because they're all quite mad, and if anyone finds out about them, we'll lose prestige, and besides they're a nuisance."

42

He found himself out of breath after the long string of phrases, and he stopped for a second. "There isn't a sane person on this planet, which isn't strange because all the 4-Fs were left when our ancestors took to space. In the eleven hundred years we've been running the Galaxy, these Crackpots have created a culture of imbecility for themselves. The Watcher garrison is maintained, to make sure the lunatics don't escape and damage our position with the other worlds around us.

"If you have a black-sheep relative, you either put him away under sur-veillance so he can't bother you, or you have him exterminated. Since we aren't barbarians like the Earthmen, we keep the madmen here, and watch them full time."

He stopped, realizing he had covered the subject quite well, and because he saw the sour expression on Furth's face.

"That's what they taught you at Academy-Central?" asked the senior Watcher.

"That's about it, except that Watcher units are all over the Galaxy, from Penares to Kyba, from the home planet to our furthest holding, doing a job for which they were trained and which no other order could do. Performing an invaluable service to all Kyben, from Kyben-Central outward to the edges of our exploration."

"Then don't you ever forget it, hear?" snapped Furth, leaning quickly across to the younger man. "Don't you ever let it slip out of your mind. If anything happens while you're awake and on the scene, and you miss it, no matter how insignificant, you'll wind up in the Mines." As if to illustrate his point, he clicked the dictobox to "on" and spoke briefly into it, keeping his eyes on a girl neatly pouring the contents of a row of glasses on the bar's floor and eating the glasses, all but the stems, which she left lying in an orderly pile.

He concluded, and leaned back toward Themus, pointing a stubby finger. "You've got a soft job here, boy. Ten years as a Watcher and you can retire. Back to a nice cozy apartment in a Project at Kyben-Central or any other planet you choose, with anyone you choose, doing anything you choose— within the bounds of the Covenant, of course. You're lucky you made it into the Corps. Many a mother's son would *give* his mother to be where you are."

He lifted the helix glass to his lips and drained it.

Themus sat, scratched his nose, and watched the purple liquid disappear.

It was his first day on Kyba, his Superior had straightened him out, he knew his place, he knew his job. Everything was clean and top-notch.

Somehow he was miserable.

Themus looked at himself. At himself as he knew he was, not as he thought he was. This was a time for realities, not for wishful thinking.

He was twenty-three, average height, blue hair, blue eyes, light complexion—just a bit lighter than the average gold-color of his people—superior intelligence, and with the rigid, logical mind of his kind. He was an accepted Underclass member of the Watcher Corps with a year of intern work at Penares Base and an immediate promotion to Kyba, which was acknowledged the soft spot before retirement. For a man as new to the Corps as Themus's five years made him, this was a remarkable thing, and explainable only by his quick and brilliant dictographic background.

He was a free man, a quick man with a dictobox, a good-looking man, and, unfortunately, an unhappy man.

He was confused by it all.

His summation of himself was suddenly shattered by the rest of his squad's entrance into the common room, voices pitched on a dozen different levels.

They came through the sliding doors, jostling and joking with one another, all tall and straight, all handsome and intelligent.

"You should have seen the one I got yesterday," said one man, zipping up his chest armor. "He was sitting in the Dog's Skull—you know, that little place on the corner of Bremen and Gabrett—with a bowl of noodle soup in front of him, tying the things together." The rest of the speaker's small group laughed uproariously. "When I asked him what he was doing, he said, 'I'm a noddle-knitter, stupid.' *He* called *me* stupid! A noodle-knitter!" He elbowed the Underclassman next to him in the ribs and they both roared with laughter.

Across the room, strapping his dictobox to his chest, one of the elder Underclassmen was studiously holding court.

"The worst ones are the psychos, gentlemen. I assure you, from six years' service here, that they take every prize ever invented. They are destructive, confusing, and elaborate to record. I recall one who was stacking *juba*-fruits in a huge pyramid in front of the library on Hemmorth Court. I watched him for seven hours, then suddenly he leaped up, bellowing, kicking the whole thing over, threw himself through a shop front, attacked a woman shopping in the store, and finally came to rest exhausted in the gutter. It was a twenty-eight-minute record, and I assure you it stretched my ability to quick-dictate. If he had ..."

Themus lost the train of the fellow's description. The talks were going on all over the common room as the squad prepared to go out. His was one of three hundred such squads, all over the city, shifted every four hours of the thirty-two-hour day, so there was no section of the city left untended. Few, if any, things escaped the notice of the Watcher Corps.

He pulled on his soft-soled jump-boots, buckled his dictobox about him, and moved into the briefing room for instructions.

The rows of seats were fast filling up, and Themus hurried down the aisle.

44

Furth, dressed in an off-duty suit of plastic body armor with elaborate scrollwork embossed on it, and the traditional black great cape, was seated with legs neatly crossed at the front of the room, on a slightly raised podium.

Themus took a seat next to the Watcher named Elix, one who had been chortling over an escapade with a pretty female Crackpot. Themus found himself looking at the other as though he were a mirror image. *Odd how so many of us look alike,* he thought. Then he caught himself. It was a ridiculous thought, and an incorrect one, of course. It was not that they looked alike, it was merely that the Kyben had found for themselves a central line, a median, to which they conformed. It was so much more logical and rewarding that way. If your brother looks and act as you do, you can predict him. If you can predict him, efficiency will follow.

Only these Crackpots defied prediction. Madmen!

"There are two current items on our order of business today, gentlemen," Furth announced, rising.

Note pads and styli appeared as though by magic, but Furth shook his head and indicated they were not needed.

"No, these aren't memoranda, gentlemen. The first is a problem of discipline. The second is an alert." There was a restless murmur in the room, and Themus glanced around to see uneasiness on many faces. What could it be?

"The problem of discipline is simply—" he pointed at Elix seated beside Themus, "—such of your Underclassmen as Watcher Elix."

Elix rose to attention.

"Pack your gear, Watcher Elix, you leave for Kyben-Central this afternoon."

Themus noted with fascination that the Watcher's face turned a shade paler.

"M-may I ask why, Superior Furth?" Elix gasped out, maintaining Corps protocol even through his panic.

"Yes, yes, of course," replied Furth in a casual, matter-of-fact manner. "You were on the scene of an orgy in the Hagars Building yesterday during second shift, were you not?"

Elix swallowed with difficulty and nodded yes, then, catching himself, he said, "Yes, Superior Furth."

"How much of that orgy did you record?"

"As much as I could before it broke up, sir."

"What you mean is, as much as you could before you found that fondling a young woman named Guzbee was more interesting than your on-duty job. Correct?"

"She—she just *talked* to me for a short time, Superior; I recorded the entire affair. It was—"

"*Out!*" Furth pointed toward the door to the common room. Elix slumped visibly, turned out of the row, walked up the aisle, and out of the briefing room.

45

"And let that be an indication, gentlemen, that we will tolerate no activities with these people, be they Kyben or not. We are here to watch, and there are enough female Watchers and Central personnel so that any desires that may be aroused in you may be quenched without recourse to our wards. Is that quite clear, gentlemen?"

He did not wait for an answer. They knew it was clear, and he knew it was clear. The message had been transmitted in the most readily understood manner.

"Now to the other business at hand," continued Furth. "We are currently looking for a man named Boolbak, who, we are told, pinches steel. I have no explanation of this description, gentlemen, merely that he 'pinches steel.'

"I can tell you that he has a big, bushy white beard, what they call twinkling eyes, a puffy-cheeked face and a scar across his forehead from temple to temple. He weighs something between 190 and 200 pounds, fat and short, and always dresses in a red jacket and knickers with white fur on them.

"If you see this man, you are to follow him, dictograph him completely—*completely*, do you understand?—and not lose sight of him unless you are relieved by at least ten other Watchers. Is that clear?"

Again he did not wait for an answer, but snapped his fingers casually, indicating the daily briefing was over.

Themus rose with the other thirty-eight Watchers and began to leave the room. There was a uniform look on all their faces; they all had the picture of Elix behind their eyes. Themus began to edge out of his row. He started when Furth called to him.

"Oh, Watcher Themus, I'd like a word with you."

Furth was a strange man, in many ways. He did not fit Themus's picture of a Superior, from previous experience with them, and, still bewildered by the abrupt fate assigned Elix, he found himself looking on his Superior with a mixture of awe, incredulousness, hatred, and fear.

"I hope the—uh—little lesson you saw today will not upset you. It was a harsh measure, to be sure, but it was the only way to get the point across."

Themus knew precisely what the Superior Watcher meant, for he had been taught from youth that this was the way matters should be handled. He also knew what he felt, but he was Kyben, and Kyben know their place.

Furth looked at him for a long moment, then pulled the black sheen that was his cloak closer about him. "I have you slated for big things here, Themus. We will have a post open for a new Junior Watcher in another six to eight months, and your record indicates you're a strong possibility."

Themus was shocked at the familiarity in both conversation protocol and exposition of Corps business, but he kept the astonishment from showing on his face.

"So I want you to keep an eye open here in Valasah," continued Furth. "There are a number of—well—irregularities we want to put a stop to."

"What sort of irregularities, Superior?" The Superior's familiarities had caused a corresponding ease to settle over the Underclassman.

"For one, this fraternization—oh, strictly on an 'occupying troops' level, to be sure, but still a deviation from the norm—and another is that we've had a number of men leave the Corps."

"You mean sent home or—like Watcher Elix?"

The Superior squirmed visibly. "Well, no, not exactly. What I mean is, they've—you might say disappeared."

Themus's eyes opened wider in surprise. "Disappeared? That indicates free choice."

The roles of Superior and Underclassman seemed for the moment to have been transposed, as Furth tried to explain to the new Watcher. "They've just gone. That's all. We can't find any trace of them. We suspect the Crackpots have been up to tricks more annoying than usual."

He suddenly stopped, realizing he had lowered himself by explaining to a lesser, and drew himself erect.

"But then, there's always been a certain percentage of loss here. Unusual, but not too unusual. This is a mad world, don't forget."

Themus nodded.

"But then, to compensate, there are a certain number of Crackpots who want to leave their insane people, also. We take off a good three hundred every year; people with the proper Kyben mind, the kind who can snap into a problem and solve it in no time. Good, logical thinkers. The administrative type. You know."

"I see, sir," said Themus, not at all understanding.

He was becoming more and more lost in trying to fathom his Superior.

The elder Watcher seemed to sense a change in the Underclassman's attitude, for once again he became brusque, realizing he had overstepped himself.

"Well, accurate snooping to you. Good rounds!"

Themus snapped a brisk salute at the Superior and left quickly.

His beat that day was the Seventh Sector, a twelve-block coverage with five fellow Watchers, their rounds overlapping. It was a route from the docks to the minaret village. From the stock pens near the Golwal Institute to the pueblo city.

Valasah, like all cities on Kyba, was a wild melange of disorder. Airy, fragile towers of transparent plastic rose spiraling next to squat quonset buildings. Teepees hunkered down next to buildings of multidimensional eccentricity, whose arms twisted in on themselves till the eye lost the track of their form.

47

Streets twisted and suddenly opened onto others. Many stopped dead as though their builders had tired of the effort of continuing. Large empty lots stood next to stores in which customers fought to get at the merchandise.

The people strutted, capered, hobbled, marched, and walked backward on both hands and feet through the streets, in the stores, across the tops of a hundred different styles of transportation.

Themus snapped his dictobox on and spoke "Record" into it. Then he walked slowly down one street, up the next, into an office building, through doors, past knots of people, dictating anything and everything. Occasionally he would see a fellow Watcher and they would exchange salutes, eyes never leaving their wards.

The Crackpots seemed oblivious to his presence. No conversation would slow or halt at his approach, no one would move from his path, all seemed to accept him somehow.

This bothered Themus.

Why aren't they angry at our eavesdropping? he wondered. *Why do they tolerate us so? Is it fear of the Kyben might? But they are Kyben, too. They call us Stuffed Shirts, but they are still Kyben. Or were once. What happened to the Kyben might that was born into each of them?*

His thoughts were cut off by sight of an old woman, skin almost yellow-white from age, rapidly wielding a three-pronged pickax at the cement of a gutter. He stopped, began dictating, and watched as she broke through the street, pulling out huge gouts of cement work and dirt from underneath. In a moment she was down on hands and knees, feverishly digging with her gnarled old hands at the dirt.

After thirty-nine minutes, her hands were raw and bleeding, the hole was quite four feet deep, and she kneeled in it, dirt arcing away into the air.

The fifty-minute mark brought her to a halt. She climbed laboriously out of the six-foot hole, grabbed the pickax and leaped back in. Themus moved nearer the edge. She was hacking away madly at a sewer pipe some three feet thick.

In a few moments she had driven a gaping hole in the side of the pipe. She reached into her bodice and brought out a piece of what looked like dirty oilcloth, strung with wires.

Themus was astounded to see both clear water and garbage running out of the pipe. Both were running together. No, they *looked* as though they were running together, but the flow of clean water came spurting out in one direction, while the muck and garbage sprayed forth from the opposite direction. They were running in opposite directions in the same pipe!

She clamped the oilcloth onto the pipe, immediately stopping the escape of the water and refuse, and began filling the hole in. Themus watched her till the hole was neatly packed in, only slightly lower than the street level. She had thrown dirt haphazardly in all directions, and some of it was still evident on car tops and in doorways.

His curiosity could be contained no longer.

He walked over to the old woman, who was slapping dirt off her polka-dotted dress, getting spots of blood on it from her rawed hands. "Excuse me—" he began.

The old woman's face suddenly assumed "Oh no, here they are again!" as its message in life.

"Garbage runs with the drinking water?" He asked the question tremulously, thinking of all the water he had drunk since his arrival, of the number of deaths from botulism and ptomaine poisoning, of the madness of these people.

The old woman muttered something that sounded like "Cretinous Stuffed Shift," and began to pick up a bag of groceries obviously dumped in a hurry before the excavating began.

"Are there many deaths from this?" Themus asked, knowing it was a stupid question, knowing the figures must be staggering, wondering if he would be one of the statistics.

"Hmmph, man, they don't even bother up and back to flow that way in negative polarization of the garboh, let me away from this maniac!" And she stalked off, dirt dropping in small clots from her polka-dotted dress.

He shook his head several times, trying to clear it, but the buzzing of his brains trying to escape through his ears prevented any comfort. He communicated her passage out of his sight through the Communicator-Attachment, received the word she had been picked up by someone else, and started to make his rounds again.

He stopped in mid-stride. It dawned on him suddenly: why hadn't that bit of oilcloth been squirted out of the hole from the pressure in the pipe? What had held it on?

He felt his tongue begin to swell in his mouth, and he realized it had all been deceiving. There had been wires attached to that scrap of oilcloth, they had served some purpose. Undoubtedly, that was it. Undoubtedly.

His fine Kyben mind pushed the problem aside.

He walked on, watching, recording. With a sudden headache.

The afternoon netted a continuous running commentary on the ordinary mundane habits of the Crackpots (biting each other on the left earlobe, which seemed to be a common activity; removing tires from landcars and replacing them with wadded-up articles of clothing; munching loaves of the spiral Kyben bread on the streets; poking long sticks through a many-holed board, to no visible purpose), and several items that Themus considered offbeat even for these warped members of his race:

49

Item: a young man leaped from the seventeenth story of an office building, plummeted to the third, landed on an awning, and after bouncing six times, lowered himself off the canvas, through the window, into the arms of an attractive blond girl holding a stenographic pad, who immediately threw the pad away and began kissing him. He did not seem to be hurt by the fall or the abrupt landing. Themus was not sure whether they had been total strangers before the leap, but he did record a break in their amours when his Audio Pickup caught her panting, "What was the name?"

Item: a blind beggar approached him on the street, crying for alms, and when he reached into a pocket to give the fellow a coin, the beggar drew himself taller than Themus had thought he could, and spat directly onto Themus's jump-boots. "Not *that* coin, you clod, not *that* coin. The *other* one." Themus was amazed, for he had but two coins in his pocket and the one intended had been a silver half-kyle and the one the beggar seemed to want was a copper nark. The beggar became indignant at the delay and hurried away, carefully sidestepping a group of men who came hurrying out of an alley.

Item: Themus saw a woman in a televiz booth, rapidly erasing the wall. Viz numbers left there by a hundred occupants suddenly disappeared under the woman's active hands. When she had the walls completely bare she reached into a bag at her feet and brought out a tube of spray paint.

In a few minutes the booth was repainted a cherry pink, and was completely dry.

Then she began writing new numbers in. After an hour and a quarter, she left, and Themus did too.

Item: a young woman lowered herself by her legs from the sign above a bar-and-grill, swinging directly into Themus's path.

Even upside down she looked good to Themus. She was wearing a pretty print dress and lavender lace undies. Themus averted his eyes and began to step around her.

"Hello," she said.

Themus stopped and found himself looking up at her, hanging by her knees from the wooden sign that said, YOU CAN EAT HERE TOO!

She was a beautiful girl, indeed; bright blue hair, a fair golden complexion, high cheekbones, lovely legs, delightful—

He drew himself to attention, turning his eyes slightly away from her, "Watcher Themus at your service, Miss."

"I like you," she said.

"Ummm?" asked Themus, not quite believing he had heard her correctly.

"Do I stutter?"

"Oh—*no*—certainly *not!*"

"Then you heard what I said."

"Well, yes, I suppose I did."

"Then why ask me to repeat it?"

"Because—because—you just *don't* come down that way and tell someone you like them. It isn't—it isn't—well, it isn't—it just isn't *ladylike!*"

She did a double flip in the air and came down lightly on the balls of her feet, directly in front of the Watcher. "Oh, swizzlegup! It's ladylike if I want to do it. If you can't tell I'm a lady just from looking at me, then I'd better find someone who can tell the difference between the sexes."

Themus found himself quite enthralled. Somehow she was not like the rest of the mad inhabitants of this world. She talked logically—although a bit more forwardly than what he had become accustomed to—and she was certainly delightful to look at. He began to ask her name, when a clear, bright picture of the damned Elix came to him. He turned to leave.

She grabbed him roughly by the sleeve, her fingernails tinkling on his armor. "Wait a minute, where are you going? I'm not finished talking to you."

"I can't talk to you. The Superior doesn't approve." He nervously ran a hand across the bridge of his nose, while looking up and down the street for brother Watchers.

"Oh, urbbledooz! Him!" She giggled. "He doesn't like anything, that's his job. *If you have a job to do, do it, you understand?*" She mimicked Furth's voice faithfully, and Themus grinned in spite of himself. She seized on his gesture of pleasure and continued, hurriedly, "I'm nineteen. My name is Darfla. What's yours, Themus?"

"I've got to go. I'll be sent to the Mines. This isn't part of my job. I've got to Watch, don't you under—"

"Oh, all right! If I make it part of your stupid Stuffed-Shirt job, will you talk to me?" She drew him into a wide, shadowed doorway with much difficulty.

"Well, I don't know how you can make it a part of my—" He looked about him in apprehension. Could he be court-martialed just for talking? Was he doomed already?

She cut in, "You're looking for a man named Boolbak, aren't you?"

"How did you—"

"Are you are you are you are you are you are you?"

"Yes, *yes*, stop that! I don't know how you found out, but yes, we are, why?" Oddly, he found himself slipping into the running-away speech of these people, and it was both pleasing and distressing. He was somehow afraid he might be going native. *But in less than two days?*

"He's my uncle. Would you like to meet him?"

"Record!" Themus barked at his dictobox.

"Oh, *must* you?" Darfla looked toward the twin suns and crossed her arms in exasperation.

51

Themus's brow furrowed and he reluctantly muttered "Off" into the box. "I'm a Watcher, and that's what I'm supposed to do. Watch. But if I don't record it all, then they can't send it to Kyben-Central and there won't be any tapes for me, and I'll get sent to the Mines." He stopped, then added, with a finger stiffly pointed between her eyebrows, "And that may not bother *you*, but I've seen reels of the Mines and crawling through a bore shaft not much wider than your body, dragging an ore sack tied to your leg, and the chance that sterility won't have time to hit before your face just ups and falls off, well, it sort of makes me worry."

He looked at her, surprised. She was tinkling. Her laughter was actually a tinkle, falling lightly from her and pleasantly tingling his ears. "What are you laughing at?" he frowned, trying to be angry though her laughter made him feel lighter than he had since he'd hit this madball world.

"Your face *ups* and *falls off!*" She laughed again. "That's the kind of thing you Stuffed Shirts would expect *me* to say! Beautiful! Yes, I'm sure I like you."

The underclass Watcher was confused. He looked about in confusion, feeling distinctly as though he had come in during the middle of a conversation. "I—I'd better be going. I don't think I want to meet your—"

"All right, all right. Suppose I fix your stupid box so it keeps right on recording; recording things that are happening, in your voice, without your being here, then would you leave it and come with me?"

"Are you out of your mind?" he yelled in a hushed tone.

"Certainly," she said, smiling broadly.

He turned once more to leave, angry and annoyed at her making fun of him. Again she stopped him.

"No, I'm sorry. Please, I can do it. Honestly. Here, let me have it."

"Look, I *can't* give you my dictobox. That's about the most terrible thing a Watcher can do. I'd be—I'd be—they'd hang me, shoot me, starve me, kill me, then send the ashes of my cremated stump to our Mines to be used for feeding the slave apes. Leave me alone!" The last was a rising note, for the girl had lifted her skirt and drawn a curved knife from her garter belt and was determinedly prying off the top of the dictobox, still attached to Themus's chest.

The Watcher fought down a mad impulse to ask her why she was wearing a garter belt when she wasn't wearing hose, and tried to stop her.

"Wait! Wait! They'll throw me out of the Corps. Stop! Here, let go there, wait a minute, I say waitaminute-forgod's sake, if you won't stop, at least let me take it off so you don't slice my throat. Here."

He slipped the shoulder straps off and unbuckled the belt. The dictobox fell into the girl's hand and she set to work fumbling about in the machine's intricate innards.

Finally she stood up, her feet lost in a pile of wirespools, vacuum tubes, metal separators, punch circuits, and plastic coils. The box looked empty inside, except for a strangely flotsamlike construction in one corner.

"Look what you've done now!"

"Stop whining, man! It's all right."

"If it's all right, make it record and play back for me." He was terrified, indignant, furious, and interested, all at once.

"I can't."

"Whaaaaaaat!"

"Why should I? I'm crazy, remember?"

Themus felt his face turn to lava. "Damn you! Look what you've done to me! In five minutes you've taken me from my Corps and sentenced me to a life that may be no longer than all the brains you have, stretched end to end!"

"Oh, stop being so melodramatic." She was smiling, tinkling again. "Now you can come with me to meet my uncle. There's no reason why you should stay here. There is a chance the box will play, if you come back to it later, as I said it would. But even if it doesn't, staying here is no help, since it isn't functioning. I'll get a mechanic to fix it, if that will make you any happier."

"No Crackpot mechanic can fix that, you fool! It's a masterpiece of Kyben science. It took hundreds of men thousands of hours to arrive at this—Oh, what's the use!" He sat down in the doorway, head in his hands.

Somehow, her logic was sound. If the box was broken, there was no reason for his refusing to go with her, for staying there could only bring him trouble sooner. It was sound, yes, but only sound on the muggy foundation of her ruining the machine in the first place. He was beginning to feel like a *tompora* snake—the kind that swallows its own tail. He didn't know which end was which.

"Come with me." Her voice had suddenly lost its youthful happiness. It was suddenly strong, commanding. He looked up.

"Get on your feet!"

He arose slowly.

"Now, come with me. If you want to come back to your box, it will be here, and it will work. Right now it will do as well if you believe I'm mad and ruined your dictobox." She jerked her head sharply toward the street. "Come on. Perhaps you can reinstate yourself by finding the man named Boolbak."

It was hopeless there among the remnants of the dictobox. There was a chance the girl wasn't as totally insane as she seemed and she actually might he Boolbak's niece. And, somehow, against all his better, stricter reasoning to the contrary, her logic was queerly sound. In a fugitive sort of way.

He went with her.

(Wondering if he was insane himself.)

53

Themus followed the girl through sections of the city Superior Furth had missed during his guided tour of inspection. They passed under a beautifully filigreed arch into a gardened street lined with monstrous blossoms growing to heights of eight and nine feet on either side of the road, casting twin shadows from the bright suns above.

Once he stopped her in the shadows of a towering flower and asked, "Why did you decide you wanted me to meet your uncle?"

"I've been watching you all day," she said simply, as if prepared to leave that as a total explanation.

"But why me?"

"I like you," she said, as though being purposely repetitious to impress him. Themus distinctly got the idea she was treating him as she would a very young child.

"Oh. I see," he said, more baffled than before. They continued down the street through an area covered by long, low structures that might have been factories were it not for the impossibly tall and spindly-looking towers that reared from the roof of each one. Themus shaded his eyes from the glare of the twin suns as he sought to glimpse what was at the top of each tower. He could see nothing.

"What are those?" he asked. He was surprised to hear his own voice. It sounded like that of an inquisitive little boy.

"Quiet, you."

That was the last thing Darfla said till they came out of nowhere and grabbed her and Themus.

Before the Watcher knew what was happening, a horde, more men than he could count, had surrounded them. They were dressed in everything from loincloth and top hat to burnoose and riding boots. Darfla gave one sharp, tiny squeal and then let her hands fall limply to her sides.

"All right, you want your say, so say!" Anger and annoyance fluttered in her voice.

A short, pock-faced man wearing a suit that appeared to be made from ropes of different colors stepped forward.

"We thought negative (click-click!) and wanted to talk on this at Cave (click-click!)." Themus listened with growing amazement. Not only did the man intersperse every few words with a metallic, unnerving tongue-clacking, but he said the word "Cave" with a low, mysterious, important tone totally unlike the rest of his speech, which was quite flat and uninflected.

Darfla raised her hands, palms upward, in resignation. "What can I say, Deere, after I say I'm sorry?"

The man addressed as Deere shook his head and said, "(Click-click!) we before talked and him not now *never never never!* Nothing to say against the

54

(Click!) but he's def but def a stuffed one at least well now for a time (Click!). Cave." Same clucking, same cryptic tone when speaking of the Cave. Themus began to worry in direct proportion to the number of surrounders.

"Let's go," Darfla said over her shoulder to Themus, not taking her eyes from Deere.

"W-where?" trembled Themus.

"Cave. Where else?"

"Oh, nowhere—I guess." He tried to be lighthearted about it. Somehow, he failed miserably.

They started off, the surrounders doing a masterful job of surrounding; cutting Themus and the girl off from anyone who might be looking. They were a walking camouflage.

Darfla began to needle Deere with caustic and, to Themus, cryptic remarks. Deere looked about to turn and put his pudgy fist in her face, and Themus nudged the girl to stop.

"Woof woof a goldfish," she tossed off as a final insult.

"(Click!)" answered Deere, sticking his tongue out.

It was a huge, featureless block in the midst of completely empty ground. Something about it suggested that it was an edifice of total disinterest. Themus recalled buildings he had seen in his youth that had been vaguely like this one. Buildings he would make a point of not bothering to enter, so uninteresting were they.

Inside it was a cave.

Stalactites hung down from the ceiling in wedge-shaped rockiness. Stalagmites pushed their way up from the floor, spiking the stone underfoot. A mud collar surrounded a small pool in which clear water rippled. The walls were hewn out of rock, the floor was sand-covered stone.

They could have been five miles underground. It was another world.

It was crammed with Crackpots.

Themus walked between two huge men wearing fezzes and sword belts, behind the clicking Deere and next to Darfla, who looked uneasy. Themus felt more than merely uneasy. He was terrified.

"Deere!"

It was Darfla. She had stopped, was being pushed unwillingly by the weight of people moving behind her. "I want this talked out right now. Here. Now. Here. Now. Here. Now—"

"Don't (Click!) try that here, Darfla. We have ours, too, you know (Click-click!)."

"All right. Straight, then."

"Were you taking him to see Boolbak?"

"Yes, why?"

"You know your uncle isn't reliable. He could say anything, Darfla. We have no fear, really, but why tempt the Chances." He pursed his pudgy lips and said, "We'll have to recondition your Watcher, girl. I'm sorry." There was a murmur from the large, restless crowd.

Themus did not know what reconditioning was, nor what the whole conversation had been about, nor who these people were, but he recognized the Watcher part, and the fact that something unpleasant was about to happen to him.

He looked around for a way out, but there was none. He was effectively manacled by the sheer weight of numbers. The Cave was filled, and the walls were lined with people. All they had to do was move in and he'd be squashed.

He remained very still, turned his inward eyes upward and ran painstakingly over the list of his family Lords, offering up to each of them paeans of praise and pleas for help and deliverance.

"No, no!" Darfla was pleading, "He's not really. He's a Kyben. I wouldn't have been able to stand him, would I, if he were a real Stuff?"

Deere bit the inside of his cheek in thought. "We thought so, too, when we got the list, but since he's been here, it's been too early to tell, and now you've let him too close to it all. We don't like this, Darfla, but—"

"Test him. He'll show you." She was suddenly close to Deere, his hand in hers, her face turned down to the fat little man's pudgy stare. "Please, Deere. For what uncle used to be."

Deere exhaled fully, pursed his lips again and said, "All right, Darfla. If the others say it's all right. It's not my decision to make."

He looked around. There was a mutter of assent from the throng. Deere turned to Themus, looking at the Watcher appraisingly.

Then suddenly—

"Here it is: we're mad. You must prove to us *you* are mad. You must do— oh, let's see—five mad acts. Truly mad. Right here in the Cave. You can do anything but harm one of us or try to escape. And we're mad, so we'll know if they're mad acts or not. Now, go on."

"Tell him the rest, Deere, tell him—" Darfla began.

"Quiet, woman! That's all there is, Watcher. Go on." He stood back, arms folded across his round little belly.

"Mad? What kind of madness? I mean, like what? I don't ... I can't do any ..." Themus looked at Darfla. Something unhinged within him at sight of her, about to cry.

He thought for a while. The crowd became impatient, voices called out things from the pack. He thought longer. Then his face smiled all the way from his mouth to his hairline.

Calmly he walked over to Darfla and began undressing her.

The clack of jaws falling was an audible thing in the sudden silence of the Cave.

Themus stripped her piece by piece, carefully knotting and pulling each piece of clothing before he went on to the next. Blouse. Knot and pull tight. Belt. Knot and pull tight. Skirt. Knot and pull tight.

Darfla offered no resistance, but her face went stoney and her jaw muscles worked rhythmically.

Eventually she was naked to the skin.

Themus bent down, made sure each item of clothing was securely knotted. Then he gathered it all up in a bundle and brought the armful to the girl. She put out her arms and he dropped the bundle into them.

"Knots to you," he said.

"One," said Deere.

Themus could feel small generators in his head begin to spin, whirr, and grind as they worked themselves up to a monstrous headache.

He stood spraddle-legged in the open area among the Crackpots, a tall, blue-haired man with a nose just a trifle too long and cheeks just a trifle too sunken, and rubbed his a-trifle-too-long nose in deep concentration.

Again he smiled.

Then he spun three times on his toes, badly, and made a wild dash for one of the onlookers.

The Crackpot looked around in alarm, saw his neighbors smiling at his discomfort, and looked back at Themus, who had stopped directly in front of him.

The Crackpot wore a shirt and slacks of motley, a flat mortarboard-type hat askew over his forehead. The mortarboard slipped a fraction of an inch as he looked at Themus.

The Watcher stood before him, intently staring at his own hand. Themus was clutching his left elbow with his right hand. His left hand was extended, the fingers bent up like spikes, to form a rough sort of enclosure.

"See my guggle fish?" asked Themus.

The Crackpot opened his mouth once; strangled a bit, closed his mouth, strangled a bit, opened his mouth again. Nothing came out.

Themus extended his hand directly under the other's nose. It was obviously a bowl he was holding in his hand. "See my guggle fish?" he repeated.

Confused, the Crackpot managed to say, "W-*what* g-guggle fish? I don't see any fish."

"That isn't odd," said Themus, grinning, "they all died last week."

Over the roar of the crowd the voice of a blocky-faced man next to the motley wearer rose:

"I see your guggle fish. Right there in the bowl. *I* see them. Now what?"

57

"You're crazier than I am," said Themus, letting the mythical bowl evaporate as he opened his hand, "I don't have any bowl."

"Two," said Deere, his brow furrowed.

Without wasting a moment, Themus began shoving the Crackpots toward the wall. Without resistance they allowed themselves to be pushed a bit. Then they stopped.

"For this one I'll need everyone's help," said Themus. "Everybody has to line up. I need everyone in a straight line, a real straight line." He began shoving again. This time they all allowed themselves to be pushed into a semblance of order, a line straight across the Cave.

"No, no," muttered Themus slowly, "that isn't quite good enough. Here." He went to one end, began moving each Crackpot a bit forward or backward till they were all approximately in the same positions of the line.

He went to the right end and squinted down the line.

"You there, fourth from the end, move back a half step, will you. Uh, yes, that's—just—*stop!* Fine. Now you," he pointed to a fellow with yellow bagged-out trousers and no shirt, "move up just a smidgee-un-uh-nuh! *Stop!* That's just perfect."

He stepped back away from them and looked along both ways, surveying them as a general surveys his troops.

"You're all nicely in line. All the same. The Crackpots are neatly maneuvered into being regimented Stuffed Shirts. Thank you," he said, grinning widely.

"Three," said Deere, blushing and furrowed at the same time.

Themus was pacing back and forth by the time the crowd had hurriedly and self-consciously gotten itself out of rank and clumped around the Cave again.

He paced from one huge stalagmite, kicking it, on turning, to the edge of the mud-surrounded pool, and began scrabbling in the mud at his feet.

He scooped up two huge handfuls of the runny stuff and carried it a few feet away to a rock surface. Plunking it down, he hurried back for another handful. This he carried with wild abandon, spraying those near him with drops of the gunk, till he was back where he had deposited the previous load. Then he stopped, considered for a long moment, then placed the mud gingerly atop the other, at an angle.

Then he hurried back for more.

This he again placed with careful deliberation, tongue poking from a corner of his mouth, eyes narrowed in contemplation.

Then another load.

And another.

Each one placed with more care than the last, till he had a huge structure over four feet tall.

He stepped back from it, looked at it, raised his thumb and squinted at it through one eye. Then he raced back to the deep hole that had been gouged out of the mud and took a fingerful of the stuff.

He ran back, patted it carefully into place, smoothed it with an experienced hand, and stepped back, with a sigh and a look of utter contentment and achievement.

"Ah! Just the way I wanted it," he said ...

... and jumped into the hole.

"Four," said Deere, tears of laughter streaming down his cheeks.

Themus sat in the hole, legs drawn up and crossed, hands cupping his chin, elbows on knees. He sat.

And sat longer.

And still sat.

And remained seated.

Deere walked over to him and looked down. "What is the fifth act of madness?"

"There isn't any."

More quickly than anyone could follow, he had swiveled back and his head had revolved on his head in a blur, *"There isn't any?"*

"I'm going to sit here and not do any more."

The crowd murmured again. "What?" cried Deere. "What do you mean, you won't do any more? We set you five. You've done four. Why no fifth?"

"Because if I don't do a fifth, you'll kill me, and I think that's mad enough even for you."

Though Deere's back was turned and he was walking away, Themus was certain he heard "Five" from somewhere.

"They want you to come back here again after you've seen my uncle," said Darfla, a definite chill in her voice.

They were walking briskly down a moving traverseway, the girl a few steps ahead of the Watcher.

Themus knew he had a small problem on his hands.

"Look, Darfla, I'm sorry about that back there, but it was my life or a little embarrassment for you. It was the first thing I could bring to mind, and I had to stall for time. I'm *really* sorry, but I'm sure they've seen a woman naked before, and you must have been naked before a man before so it shouldn't—"

Themus fell silent. The continued down the traverseway, Darfla striding forward, anger evident in each long step.

Finally the girl came to an intersection of belt strips and agilely swung across till she was on the slowest-moving outer belt. She stepped off, took several rapid steps to lose momentum, and turned to Themus.

"We'd better stop in here for a moment and get you something to wear over that Watcher uniform. It isn't hard to avoid the Stuffed Shirts," she said, looking at him with disparagement, "but there's no sense taking foolish chances."

She indicated a small shop that was all window and no door, with a hastily painted message across one of the panes. ELGIS THE COSTUMER and IF WE DON'T GOT IT, IT AIN'T WORTH HAVING! They entered through a cleverly designed window that spun on a center pin.

Inside the shop Darfla spoke briefly to a tall, thin Crackpot in black half-mask and bodytight black suit. He disappeared down a shaft in the floor from which stuck a shining pole.

The girl pulled a bolt of cloth off a corner of the counter and perched herself, with trim legs crossed. Themus stood looking at the shop.

It was a costumer's all right, and with an arrangement and selection of fantastic capacities. Clothing ranged from rustic Kyben farmgarb to the latest spun plastene fibers from all over the Galaxy. He was marveling at the endless varieties of clothing when the tall, thin Crackpot slid back up the pole.

He stepped off onto the floor, much to Themus's amazement, and no elevator disc followed him. It appeared that the man had come up the pole the same way he had gone down, without mechanical assistance. Themus was long past worrying over such apparent inconsistencies. He shrugged and looked at the suit the fellow had brought up with him.

Ten minutes later he looked at the suit on himself, in a full-length mirror cube, and smiled at his sudden change from Underclass Watcher Themus to a sheeted and fetish-festooned member of the Toad Revelers cult found on Fewb-huh IV.

His earrings hung in shining loops to his shoulders, and the bag of toad shavings on his belt felt heavier than he thought it should. He pulled the drawstring on the bag and gasped. They *were* toad shavings. He tucked the bottom folds of the multicolored sheet into his boot tops, swung the lantern onto his back, and looked at Darfla in expectation.

He caught her grinning, and when he, too, smiled, her face went back to its recent stoniness.

Darfla made some kind of arrangement with Elgis, shook his hand, bit his ear, said, "How are the twins, Elgis?" to which the costumer replied, "Eh!" in a lackadaisical tone, and they left.

The rest of the trip through the patchwork quilt of Valasah was spent in silence.

The Crackpots were not what they seemed. Of that Themus was certain. He had been very stupid not to notice it before, and he thought the

Watchers must be even more stupid for not having seen it in all their hundreds of years on Kyba.

But there was a factor he did not possess. Garbage and water that ran in different directions through the same pipe, a beggar that knew how many coins he had in his pocket, a girl who could rip out the innards of a dictobox, leaving it so it would work—and somehow he was now certain it *would* work—without a human behind it, and a full-sized cave built inside a concrete block. These were not the achievements of madmen.

But they *were* mad!

They had to be. All the things which seemed mysterious and superhuman were offset by a million acts of out-and-out insanity. They lived in a world of no standardization, no conformity at all. There was no way to gauge the way these people would act, as you could with the Kyben of the stars. It was—it was—well, *insane!*

Themus's nose itched in confusion, but he refrained from unseemly scratching.

"Don't I look like Santa Claus?" he said.

"Who?" asked Themus, looking at the roly-poly florid face and bushy beard. He tried to ignore the jaggedly yellow scar that reached from temple to temple.

"Santa Claus, Santa Claus, you lout? Haven't you ever heard of the Earthmen's mythical hero, Santa Claus? He was the hero of the Battle of the Alamo, he discovered what they call the Great Pyramid of Gizeh, he was the greatest drinker of milk out of wooden shoes that planet ever knew!"

"What's milk?" asked Themus.

"Lords, what a clod!" He screwed up his lips in a childish pout. "I did immense research work on the subject. Immense!" Then he muttered, under his breath, almost an afterthought, "Immense."

The old man was frightened. It showed, even through the joviality of his garb and appearance.

Themus could not understand the old man. He looked as though he would be quite the maddest of the lot, but he talked in a soft, almost whispering voice, lucidly and, for the most part, of familiar things. Yet there was something about him which set him apart from the other Crackpots. He did not have the wild-eyed look.

No one was saying anything and the sounds of their breathing in the basement hideout was loud in Themus's ears. "Are you Boolbak, the steel pincher?" the Watcher asked, to make conversation. It seemed like the thing to say.

The bearded oldster shifted his position on the coal pile on which he was sitting, blackening his beard, covering his red suit with dust. His voice changed from a whisper to a shrill. "A spy! A spy! They've come after me.

You'll do it to me! You'll bend it! Get away from me, get away from me, gedda way from me, geddawayfromee!" The old man was peering out from over the top of the pile, pointing a shaking finger at Themus.

"Uncle Boolbak!" Darfla's brows drew down and she clapped her hands together. The old man stopped shouting and looked at her.

"What?" he asked, pouting childishly.

"He's no spy, whatever he is," she said, casting a definitely contemptuous glance at Themus. "He was a Watcher alerted to find you. I liked him," she said looking toward the ceiling to find salvation for such a foul deed, "and I thought that it was about time you stopped this nonsense of yours and spoke to one of them. So I brought him here."

"Nonsense? Nonsense, is it! Well, you've sealed my doom, girl! Now they'll bend it around your poor uncle's head as sure as Koobis and Poorah rise every morning. Oh, what have you done?"

The girl shook her head sadly, "Oh, stop it, will you. No one wants to hurt you. Show him your steel pinching."

"No!" he answered, pouting again.

Themus watched in amazement. The man was senile. He was a tottering, doddering child. Of what possible use could he be? Of what possible *interest* could he be to both the Watchers and the Crackpots who had tried to stop Darfla's bringing him here?

Suddenly the old man smiled secretly and moved in closer, sidling up to the Watcher as though he had a treasure everyone was after. He made small motions with his pudgy fingers, indicating he wanted Themus's attention, his patience, his silence, and his ear, in that order. It was a most eloquent motioning, and Themus found he was complying, though no vocal request had been made. He bent closer.

Uncle Boolbak dug into a pocket of the red coal-coated jacket, and fished out a cane-shaped, striped piece of candy. "Want a piece of candy? Huh, want it, huh?"

Themus felt an urge to bolt and run, but he summoned all his dignity and said, "I'm Themus, Underclass Watcher, and I was told you—pinch steel. Is that right?"

For a moment the old man looked unhappy that the Watcher did not want any candy, then suddenly his face hardened. The eyes lost their twinkle and looked like two cold diamonds blazing at him. Boolbak's voice, too, became harder, more mature, actually older. "Yes, that's right, I 'pinch' steel, as you put it. You wonder what that means, eh?"

Themus found himself unable to talk. The man's whole demeanor had changed. The Watcher suddenly felt like a child before a great intellect. He could only nod.

"Here. Let me show you." The old man went behind the furnace and brought out two plates of steel. From a workbench along one wall he took a metal punch and double-headed hammer. He threw down one of the plates, and handed Themus the punch and hammer.

"Put a hole in this with that punch," he said, motioning Themus toward the other plate, which he had laid flat on the workbench.

Themus hesitated. "Come, come, boy. Don't dawdle."

The Watcher stepped to the workbench, set the punch on the plate and tapped lightly till he had a hole started. Then he placed the punch in it again and brought the hammer down on its head with two swift strokes. The clangs rang loud in the dim basement. The punch sank through the plate and went a quarter-inch into the table. "I didn't hit it very hard," Themus explained, looking over his shoulder at "Santa Claus."

"That's all right. It's very soft steel. Too many impurities. Kyben spacecraft are made of a steel which isn't too much better than this, though they back it with strong reinforcers. Now watch."

He took the plate in his hand, holding it between thumb and forefinger at one corner, letting it hang down. With the other hand he pinched it at the opposite corner, pressing thumb and forefinger together tightly.

The plate crumbled to dust, drifting down over the old man's pinching hand in a bright stream.

Themus's mouth opened of its own accord, his chest tightened. Such a thing wasn't possible. The old man was a magician.

The dust glowed up at him from the floor. It was slightly luminous. He goggled, unable to help himself.

"Now," said Boolbak, taking the other plate. "Put a hole in this one."

Themus found he was unable to lift the hammer. His hands refused to obey. One did not see such things and remain untouched.

"Snap out of it, boy! Come on, punch!" The old man's voice was commanding; Themus broke his trance.

He placed the punch on the second plate and in three heavy blows had gone through it and into the table again.

"Fine, fine," said Uncle Boolbak, holding the second plate as he had the first. He pinched it, with a slight revolving movement of the fingers.

The steel seemed to change. It stayed rigid in shape, but the planes of it darkened, ran together. It was a flat piece of metal, but suddenly it seemed to have depths, other surfaces.

Boolbak held it out to Themus, "Put another hole in it."

Themus took it, wonderingly, and laid it down on the workbench. It seemed heavier than before. He brought the hammer down sharply, three times.

The metal was unmarred.

63

He set the punch and hammered again, harder, half a dozen times. He took the punch away. Its point was dulled, the punch shank was slightly bowed. The metal was unscarred.

"It's—it's—" he began, his tongue abruptly becoming a wad of cotton batting in his mouth.

Boolbak nodded, "It's changed, yes. It is now harder than any steel ever made. It can withstand heat or cold that would either melt to paste or shatter to splinters any other metal. It is impregnable. It is the ideal war metal. With it an army is invincible. It is the closest thing to an ultimate weapon ever devised, for it is unstoppable.

"A tank composed of this metal would be a fearsome juggernaut. A spaceship of it could pierce the corona of a sun. A soldier wearing body armor of it would be a superman." He stood back, his lips a thin line, letting Themus look dumbfoundedly at the plate he held.

"But how do you—how can you—it's impossible! How can you make this? What have you done to it?" Themus felt the room swirl around him, but that defied the laws of the universe.

"Sit down. I want to talk to you. I want to tell you some things." He put one arm around Themus's shoulders, leading him to a flight of stairs, to sit down.

Themus looked at Darfla. She was biting her lip. Was this the talk the Crackpots did not want him to have with Uncle Boolbak?

Themus sensed: this is it. This is an answer. Perhaps not *the* answer to all that troubled him, but it was, unquestionably, *an* answer.

Suddenly he didn't want to know. He was afraid; terribly afraid. He stammered. "Do-do you think you should? I'm a Watcher, you know, and I don't want to—"

The old man cut him off with a wave of his hand, and pushed him down firmly.

"You think you're watching us, don't you?" began Boolbak. "I mean, you think the Watcher Corps was assigned here to keep an eye on all the loonies, don't you? To keep the black sheep in the asylum so the star-flung Kyben don't lose face or esteem in the Galaxy, isn't that it?"

Themus nodded, reluctantly, not wanting to insult the old man.

Boolbak laughed. "Fool! We *want* you here. Do you think for a moment we'd allow you blundering pompous snoopers around if we didn't have a use for you?

"Let me tell you a story," the old man went on. "Hundreds of years ago, before what you blissfully call the Kyben Explosion into space, both Crackpots and Stuffed Shirts lived here, though they weren't divided that way, back then. The Stuffed Shirts were the administrators, the implements of keeping everything neatly filed, and everyone in line. That type seems to gravitate toward positions of influence and power.

64

"The Crackpots were the nonconformists. They were the ones who kept coming up with the new ideas. They were the ones who painted the great works of art. They were the ones who composed the most memorable music. They were the ones who overflowed the lunatic asylums. They thought up the great ideas, true, but they were a thorn in the side of the Stuffs, because they couldn't be predicted. They kept running off in all directions at once. They were a regimental problem. So the Stuffs tried to keep them in line, gave them tedious little chores to do, compartmentalized them in thought, in habits, in attitudes. The noncons snapped. There is no record of it, but there was almost a war on this planet that would have wiped out every Kyben—of both breeds—to the last man."

He rubbed a hand across his eyes, as if to wipe away unpleasant images.

Themus and Darfla listened, intently, their eyes fastened to those of the old man in his ridiculous costume. Themus knew Darfla must have heard the story before, but still she strained to catch every sound Boolbak made.

"Luckily, the cooler heads won. An alternate solution was presented and carried out. You've always thought the Kyben left their misfits, the Crackpots, behind. That we were left here because we weren't good enough, that we would disgrace our hard-headed pioneers before the other races, isn't that the story you've always heard? That we are the black sheep of the Kyben?"

He laughed, shaking his head.

"Fools! We threw you out! We didn't want you tripping all over our heels, annoying us. We weren't left behind—*you* were thrown away!"

Themus's breath caught in his throat. It was true. He knew it was true. He had no doubts. It was so. In the short space of a few seconds the whole structure of his life had been inverted. He was no longer a member of the elite corps of the elite race of the universe; he was a clod, an unwanted superfluousity, a tin soldier, a carbon copy.

He started to say something, but Boolbak cut him off. "We have nothing against ruling the Galaxy. We like the idea, in fact. Makes things nice when we want something unusual and it takes influence to get it quickly. But why should we bother doing the work when we can pull a string or two and one of you armor-plated puppets will perform the menial tasks.

"Certainly we allow you to rule the Galaxy. It keeps you out of trouble, and out of our hair. You rule the Galaxy, but *we* rule *you!*"

Thunder rolled endlessly through the Watcher's head. He was being bombarded with lightning, and he was certain any moment he would rip apart. It was too much, all too suddenly.

Boolbak was still talking: "We keep the Watcher Corps on other worlds both for spying purposes and as a cover-up. So we can have a Watcher Corps here on Kyba without attracting any attention to ourselves. A few hundred of

65

you aren't that much bother, and it's ridiculously easy to avoid you when we wish to. Better than a whole planet of you insufferable bores."

He stopped again, and pointed a pudgy finger at Themus's chest armor.

"We established the Watcher Corps as a liaison between us, when we had innovations, new methods, concepts ready for use, and you, with your graspy little hands always ready to accept what the 'lunatics back home' had come up with.

"Usually the ideas were put into practice and you never knew they originated here.

"We made sure the Watchers' basic motto was to watch, watch, watch, whatever we did, to save ourselves the trouble of getting the information back where it would do the most good, undistorted—and believe me, if we didn't want you to see something, it wasn't hard to hide it from you; you're really quite simple and stupid animals—so when we had a new invention or concept, all we had to do was walk into a public square and demonstrate it for you. *Pegulla*, see—*pegulla*, do."

Themus mused aloud, interrupting the old man, "But what does, well, stacking *juba*-fruits in the square demonstrate?"

"We wouldn't expect your simple-celled minds to grasp something like that immediately," answered Boolbak. "But I happen to know Shella, who did that, and I know what he was demonstrating. He was illustrating a new system of library filing, twice as efficient as the old one.

"He knew it would be dictated, sent back to Kyben-Central and finally understood for what it was. We give you enough clues. If something seems strange, think about it a while, and a logical use and explanation will appear. Unfortunately, that is the one faculty the Star-Flung Kyben are incapable of using. Their minds are patterned, their thoughts set in tracks." The laugh was a barb this time.

"But why are you all so—so—*mad?*" Themus asked, a quavering note in his voice.

"Beginning to crack, boy? I'll tell you why we're *mad*, as you put it. We're not mad, we're just doing what we want, when we want, the way we want. You rigid thinkers can't recognize the healthy sanity of that. You think everyone has to wear a standardized set of clothes, go to his dentist a specified number of times, worship in delineated forms, marry a specified type of mate. In other words, live his life in a mold.

"The only way to stimulate true creativeness is to allow it to grow unchained with restrictions. We're not mad at all. We may put on a bit, just to cover from you boobs, but we're saner than you. Can you change the molecular structure of a piece of steel, just by touching it at a juncture of atom chains?"

66

"Is that—that—how you did it?" Themus asked.

"Yes. How far could I have gotten on a thing of this kind if I'd grown up in a culture like the one you've always known?

"For every mad thing you see on this world, there is a logical, sane answer."

Themus felt his knees shaking. This was all too much to be taken at one sitting. The very fiber of his universe was being unwound and split down the grain.

He looked at Darfla for the first time in what seemed an eternity, and found it impossible to tell what she was thinking.

"Buy why haven't you shown this steel pinching to the Watchers, if you want them to know all the new concepts?" the incredulous Themus questioned.

Boolbak's face suddenly went slack. The eyes became glassy and twinkly again. His face became flushed. He clapped his hands together childishly. "Oh, no! I don't want that!"

"But why?" demanded Themus.

Again the old man's face changed. This time abject terror shone out. He began to sweat. "They're gonna chase me, and bend a bar of iron around my head."

He leaped up and ran in a flurry back to the coal pile, where he burrowed into the black dust and peered out, trembling.

"But that's crazy! No one wants to bend a bar of iron around your head. Only a maniac would keep a secret like that because of a crazy reason like that!"

"Exactly," came Darfla's voice from behind him, sadly, "that's just it. Uncle *is* crazy."

They had wanted to see Themus after his talk with Uncle Boolbak, and though Darfla had taken pains to cover their tracks, a group of Crackpots were waiting outside the house when they emerged.

Themus was white and shaking, and made no movement of resistance as they were hustled into a low-slung bubble roadster and whisked back to the Cave.

"Well, did he talk to that mad genius?" asked Deere.

Darfla nodded sullenly. "Just as you said. He knows."

Deere turned to Themus. "Not quite all, however. Do you think you can take more, Watcher?"

Themus felt distinctly faint. One microscopic bit more added to the staggering burden of revelation he had had tossed on him, and he was prepared to sink through the floor.

However, Deere was not waiting for an answer. He motioned to a man in a toga and spiked belt, who came toward Themus. "See this man?" Deere asked.

Themus said yes. Deere tapped the man lightly on the chest, "Senior Watcher, First Grade, Norsim, lately disappeared from the barracks at Kyba

Base, Valasah." He pointed to three others standing together near the front of the crowd. "Those three were top men in the Corps, over a period of ten years. Now they're Crackpots."

Themus's eyebrows and hands asked, "But how?"

"There is a gravitating factor among Kyben," he explained. "There are Crackpots who are brought up as Stuffs, who realize, when they get here, that their thinking has been fettered. Eventually they come to us. They come to us for the simple reason that the intellect rises through the Watcher ranks, and for several reasons gets assigned here. We've made sure the smartest boys get final assignment here.

"On the other side of the ledger there are noncons who go psycho from the responsibility of being a freethinker, when they want supervision and their thinking directed. They eventually wind up as Kyben, after minor reconditioning so they don't remember all this," he waved his hand to indicate the Cave. "Now they're somewhere out there and probably quite happy."

"But how can you make a Watcher disappear so completely, when the whole garrison here is looking—"

"Simple," said a voice from behind Themus.

Supervisor Furth just stood smiling.

Themus just stood choking.

The elder Watcher grinned at the confusion swirling about Themus's face.

"How did—when were you—" Themus stuttered.

Furth raised a hand to stop him. "I was an unbending Stuff for a good many years, Themus, before I realized the Crackpot in me wanted out." He grinned widely. "Do you know what did it? I was kidnapped, put in a barrel with a bunch of chattering *pegullas*, and forced to think my way out. I finally made it, and when I crawled out, all covered with *pegulla* dung, those grinning maniacs helped me up and said, 'More fun than a barrel of *pegullas!'*"

Themus began to chuckle.

"That did it," said Furth.

"But why do you send men like Elix back to the Mines? You must know how horrible it is. That isn't at all consistent."

Furth's mouth drew down at the corner. "It is, when you consider that I'm supposed to be the iron hand of the Watcher garrison here on Kyba. We have to keep the Stuffs in line. They have to be maneuvered, while they think they're maneuvering us. And Elix was getting too far out of line."

"Do you know how close to being killed you came when we brought you here the first time?" Deere said.

Themus turned back to the pock-faced little man, "No. I—I—thought you'd just send me back and let the Corps deal with me."

"Hardly. We aren't afraid of our blundering brothers with the armored hides, but we certainly don't take wide chances to attract attention to ourselves. We like our freedom too much for that.

"You see, we aren't play-acting at being odd. We actually enjoy and live the job of being individuals. But there is a logic to our madness. Nothing we do is folly."

"But," Themus objected, "what are the explanations for things like—" and he finger-listed several things that had been bothering him.

"The garbage is negatively polarized, so it touches nothing but its side of the sewer pipes," explained Furth. "The beggar, who, by the way, is a professional numismatist, can sense the 'structural aura' of various metals, that's how he knew how many and what type coins you had in your pocket. The Cave here is merely an adequate job of force-moving large areas of soil and rock, and atomic realignment ..."

He explained for a few more minutes, Themus's astonishment becoming deeper and deeper at each further revelation of what he had considered superhuman achievements. Finally, the young Watcher asked, "But why haven't these discoveries been turned over to Kyben-Central?"

"There are some things our little categorizing brothers aren't ready for, as yet," explained Deere. "Even you were not ready. Chance saved you, you know."

Themus looked startled. "Chance?"

"Well, chance and your innate intelligence, boy. We had to see if there was enough noncon in you to allow you to live. The reconditioning in your case would have been—ah—something of a failure. The five mad acts you were to perform not only had to be mad—they had to be *logically* mad. They each had to illustrate a point."

"Wait a minute," said Themus. "I had no idea what I was going to do. I just did it, that's all."

"Um-hm. Quite right, but if *you* didn't know, at least your subconscious was able to put two and two together and come up with the proper four. The acts you did demonstrated you had courage enough to be a noncon, that you were smart enough to maneuver us Crackpots—so it would be easy enough for you to help us maneuver the Stuffs—that you could be a noncon thinker when you had to be, and even you knew you were too valuable to kill.

"Even if *you* weren't in on it, your subconscious and the rest of *us* were."

"But—but—what I don't get is why did you try to stop me from seeing Boolbak and then let me go, and why does Boolbak hide from you and the Watchers both?"

"One at a time," replied Deere. "Boolbak hides because he *is* mad. There are some like that in every group. He happens to be a genius, but he's also a total madman. We don't try to keep tabs on him, because we already have the

69

inventions he's come up with, but we don't put him out of the way because he might get something new one of these days we *don't* have, and then, too, he was a great man once, long before—" He stopped suddenly, realizing he had stepped over the line from explanation to maudlinity. "We're not barbarians. Nor are we a secret underground movement. We don't want to overthrow anything, we just want to do as we please. If our brothers feel like foaming up and ruling star systems, all well and good, it makes it easier for us to obtain the things we want, so we help them in a quiet way. Boolbak isn't doing anyone any harm, but we didn't think you were ready to be exposed to too much noncon thinking all at once, as we knew Boolbak would do. He always does.

"But Darfla was so concerned, and she seemed to like you, so we took a chance. It seemed to work out, luckily for you."

Themus looked at the girl. She was staring at him as though a layer of ice covered her. He smiled to himself.

Any amount of ice can be thawed by the proper application of intensive heat.

"We didn't want you to see him at first," Deere went on, "because we knew he would dump the cart. But when you showed us you were flexible enough to do the five mad acts, we knew you could take what Boolbak had to say.

"And we let him explain it, instead of us, because he's one damned fine storyteller. He can hold the interest. He's a born minstrel and you'd believe him before us."

"But why did he tell me all that? I thought you wanted it all kept quiet? He hardly knew me and he explained the whole situation, the way it really is. Why?" Themus inquired.

"Why? Because he's completely out of his mind—and he's a big-mouth to boot," Deere stated, "We tolerate Boolbak, but we make sure he keeps away from the Watchers, for the most part. If he does get through, though, it eventually shuttles to Furth and we snap a lid on it. I suppose he was ready to tell you because Darfla brought you to him. He has a soft spot for her.

"What I want to know is, why did Darfla take you off your rounds in the first place?"

Darfla looked up. She had been idly running her toe through the mud near the pool. "I went through his dossier. He was too brilliant for the Corps. His record indicated any number of checkpoints of upper-level intelligence. So I went and found him. He didn't react as most Stuffs would have, when I applied a few stimuli, such as ruining his dictobox."

Themus winced at the memory of the dictobox.

"But what made you look up his dossier?" demanded Furth.

Darfla hesitated, and a gold blush crept up her cheeks. "I saw him get off the ship from Penares Base. I—well—I rather liked his appearance. You know." She looked down again, embarrassed.

Deere made a gun with thumb and forefinger, pointed it at her, "If you don't stop taking these things into your own hands! There's a group who looks into things like that. We'd have gotten to him in time."

Themus rubbed his nose in amazement. "I—I just can't believe all this. It's so fantastic. So unreal."

"No more unreal to believe every man is a single brain with individual thoughts than to believe he's a member of a group mind with the same thoughts for all."

He clapped the Watcher on the back.

"Are you prepared to drop your life as a Watcher and become one of us? I think you'll be quite a find. Your five acts were the maddest we've seen in a long time."

"But I'm not a Crackpot. I'm a Stuffed Shirt. I've always been one."

"Bosh! You were brought up to think you were one. We've shown you there are other ways to think, now use them."

Themus considered. He'd never really had anything, as a member of the Kyben race—the rulers of the universe—but a constant unease and a fear of the Mines. These people all seemed so free, so clever, so—so—He was at a loss for words.

"Can you take me out of sight of the Corps?" he asked.

"Easiest thing in the world," said Furth, "to make you drop out of sight as Themus, the Watcher, and make you reappear as—let's say—Gugglefish, the Crackpot Mountebank."

Themus's face broke into the first full, unreserved smile he could recall. "It's a deal, I suppose. I've always wanted to live in a madhouse. The only thing that bothers me is Uncle Boolbak. You fool the Stuffs by pretending madness, and, well—you consider Boolbak mad, so perhaps—"

He stopped when he saw the perplexed looks that came over the Crackpots' faces. It was a germ of thought.

"Welcome home, maniac," said Deere.

The pain in this one is the pain of a mind blocked from all joy and satisfaction by an outworn idea, an idée fixe, a monomaniacal hangup that tunnels the vision. Think of someone you know, even someone you love, trapped into a corrupt or self-destructive or anti-social behavior pattern by an inability to get around the roadblock of erroneous thinking. Pathetic.

The story is about a man and a woman. The woman is the good guy, the man is the dummy. When it appeared in Analog, Kelly Freas did a drawing that showed the man as the stronger of the two, his body positioned in such a way that it looked as if he was protecting the lesser female. Wrong. I tried to get Ben Bova, the editor of Analog, to get Kelly to alter the drawing, but it was too close to the publication deadline, so it went in that way.

But, much as I admire and respect Kelly, I took it not so much as a sexist attitude on his part—Polly wouldn't permit such an evil to exist—as an unconscious understanding of the massmind of the general Analog readership, which is, at core and primarily, engineers, technicians, scientists, men of the drawing board and the spanner.

So I wasn't perplexed or saddened when the story came in at the bottom of Analog's Analytical Laboratory ratings. Where else would a story that says machismo is bullshit and a woman thinks more reasonably than a man come in? Diana King at the magazine assures me the short stories always come in last, but I think she's just trying to help me over a bad time; I handle rejection, I just don't handle it well.

Nonetheless, I'm including it in this collection, an addition to the stories that appeared in previous editions of this book, not only to give you a little extra for your money, but because it's the latest in my Earth-Kyba War stories. And what with "The Crackpots" here, the first of the series, it makes a nice little package.

There's not much else to say about it. This isn't the most soul-sundering tale I've ever tried to write, it's just an attempt to do an actual, honest-to-God science fiction story for Analog. To see if I could do it on my own terms. And to see if I could gig the Analog readers of thirty-and-more years' good standing, who would have coronary arrest at seeing Ellison in the hallowed pages of their favorite magazine. You can imagine my joy when I saw the issue on the newsstands, with my name on the front cover with Isaac Asimov's, knowing that Analog's faithful would be gagging, and knowing the little jibe I had waiting for them inside with

Sleeping Dogs

The only "positive" thing Lynn Ferraro could say about the destruction of the cities of Globar and Schall was that their burning made aesthetically-pleasing smears of light against the night sky of Epsilon Indi IV.

"The stiffness of your back tells me you don't approve, Friend Ferraro." She didn't turn at his words, but she could feel her vertebrae cracking as she tensed. She kept her face turned to the screens, watching the twin cities shrink as the flames consumed them, a wild colossus whose pillared legs rose to meet a hundred meters above the debacle.

"A lot of good my disapproval does, Commander."

He made a sighing sound at her response. "Well, you have the satisfaction of knowing your report will more than likely terminate my career."

She turned on him, her facial muscles tight as sun-dried leather. "And a hell of a lot of good *that* does the people down there!"

She was an *Amicus Hostis*, a Friend of the Enemy, placed on board the Terran dreadnought *Descartes*, Solar Force registry number SFD/199–660, in this the forty-first year of the Earth-Kyba War, to prevent atrocities, to attempt *any kind* of rapprochement with the Kyben, should a situation present

75

itself in which the Kyben would do other than kill or be killed. And when it had become clear that this lunatic, this butcher, this Commander Julian Drabix was determined to take the planet—at any cost—no matter how horrifyingly high—scorched earth if nothing short of that monstrousness would suffice—when it had become clear her command powers would be ignored by him, she had filed a light-wave report with Terran Central. But it would take time for the report to reach Central, time for it to be studied, time for a report-judgment and time for instructions to be light-fired back to the *Descartes*. And Drabix had not waited. Contravening the authority of the *Amicus*, he had unleashed the full firepower of the dreadnought.

Globar and Schall burned like Sodom and Gomorrah.

But unlike those God-condemned hellholes of an ancient religion, no one knew if the residents of Globar and Schall were good, or evil, or merely frightened natives of a world caught in the middle of an interstellar war that seemed destined *never* to end.

"All I know," Drabix had said, by way of justification, "is that planet's atmospheric conditions are perfect for the formation of the crystalline form of the power-mineral we need. If we don't get it, Kyba will. It's too rare, and it's too important to vacillate. I'm sorry about this, but it has to be done." So he had done it.

She had argued that they didn't even know for certain if the mineral was *there*, in the enormous quantities Drabix believed were present. It was true the conditions were right for its formation, and on similar worlds where the conditions were approximated they had found the precious crystals in small amounts ... but how could even such a near-certainty justify destruction so total, so inhuman?

Drabix had chosen not to argue. He had made his choice, knowing it would end his career in the Service; but he was a patriot; and allegiance overrode all other considerations.

Ferraro despised him. It was the only word that fit. She despised everything about him, but this blind servitude to cause was the most loathsome aspect of his character.

And even that was futile, as Globar and Schall burned.

Who would speak the elegy for the thousands, perhaps millions, who now burned among the stones of the twin cities?

When the conflagration died down and the rubble cooled, the *Descartes* sent down its reconnaissance ships; and after a time, Commander Drabix and Friend Ferraro went to the surface. To murmur among the ashes.

Command post had been set up on the island the natives called Stand of Light because of the manner in which the sunlight from Epsilon Indi was reflected back from the sleek boles of the gigantic trees that formed a central cluster forest in the middle of the twenty-five-kilometer spot of land. Drabix had ordered his recon teams to scour the planet and bring in a wide sample of prisoners. Now they stood in ragged ranks up and down the beach as far as Lynn Ferraro could see; perhaps thirty thousand men and women and children. Some were burned horribly.

She rode on the airlift platform with Drabix as he skimmed smoothly past them, just above their heads.

"I can't believe this," Drabix said.

What he found difficult to accept was the diversity of races represented in the population sample the recon ships had brought in. There were Bleshites and Mosynichii in worn leathers from the worlds of 61 Cygni, there were Camogasques in prayer togas from Epsilon Eridani, there were Kopektans and Livides from Altair II and X; Millmen from Tau Ceti, Oldonians from Lalande 21185, Runaways from Rigel; stalk-thin female warriors of the Seull Clan from Delta Cephei III, beaked Raskkans from the hollow asteroids of the Whip belt, squidlike Silvinoids from Grover; Petokii and Vulpeculans and Rohrs and Mawawanians and creatures even Drabix's familiarity with the Ephemeris could not identity.

Yet nowhere in the thousands of trembling and cursing prisoners—watching the airlift platform as it passed them—nowhere in that horde, could be seen even one single golden-skinned, tentacle-fingered Kyben. It was this, perhaps, that Drabix found the more impossible to accept. But it was so. Of the expeditionary force sent from far Kyba to hold this crossroads planet, not one survivor remained. They had all, to the last defender, suicided.

When the knowledge could no longer be denied, Lynn turned on Drabix and denounced him with words of his own choosing, words he had frequently used to vindicate his actions during the two years she had ridden as super-cargo on the *Descartes*. "'War is not merely a political act but also a political instrument, a continuation of political relations, a carrying out of the same by other means,' as Karl von Clausewitz has so perfectly said."

He snarled at her. "Shut your face, *Amicus*! I'm not in a mood for your stupidities!"

"And slaughter is not merely an act of war, is that right, Commander? Is it *also* a political instrument? Why not take me to see the stacked corpses? Perhaps I can fulfill *my* mission ... perhaps I'll learn to communicate with the dead! You deranged fool! You should be commanding an abattoir, not a ship of the line!"

He doubled his right fist and punched her full in the face, within sight of the endless swarm of helpless prisoners and his own crew. She fell backward, off the airlift, tumbling down into the throng. Their bodies broke her fall, and within seconds members of Drabix's crew had rescued her; but he did not see

77

it; the airlift had skimmed away and was quickly lost in the flash of golden brilliance reflecting off the holy shining trees of Stand of Light.

The adjutant found her sitting on a greenglass boulder jutting up from the edge of the beach. Waves came in lazily and foamed around the huge shape. There was hardly any sound. The forest was almost silent; if there were birds or insects, they had been stilled, as though waiting.

"Friend Ferraro?" he said, stepping into the water to gain her attention. He had called her twice, and she had seemed too sunk in thought to notice. Now she looked down at him and seemed to refocus with difficulty.

"Yes, I'm sorry, what is it, Mr. Lalwani?"

"The Commander would like to see you."

Her expression smoothed over like the surface of the pale blue ocean. "Where is he?"

"On the main continent, Miz. He's decided to take the forms."

She closed her eyes in pain. "Dear souls in Hell ... will there never be an end? Hasn't he done enough to this wretched backwash?" Then she opened her eyes and looked at him closely. "What does he want with me? Has there been a reply from Central? Does he simply want an audience?"

"I don't know, Miz. He ordered me to come and find you. I have a recon ship waiting, whenever you're ready."

She nodded. "Thank you, Mr. Lalwani. I'll be along in a few moments."

He saluted and walked away up the beach and around the bend. She sat staring out across the ocean; as always: an observer.

They had charted the positions of the fifty "forts" during the first pass at the planet. Whether they were, in fact, forts was entirely supposition. At first they were thought to be natural rock formations—huge black cubes sunk into the earth of the tiny planet; featureless, ominous, silent—but their careful spacing around the equator made that unlikely. And the recon ships had brought back confirmation that they were created, not natural. *What* they were, remained a mystery.

Lynn Ferraro stood with Drabix and stared across the empty plain to the enormous black cube, fifty meters on a side. She could not remember ever having seen anything quite so terrifying. There was no reason to feel as she did, but she could not shake the oppression, the sense of impending doom. Even so, she had resolved to say nothing to Drabix. There was nothing that *could* be said. Whatever motivated him, whatever passions had come to possess him in his obsession about this planet, she knew no words she might speak to dissuade him.

"I wanted you here," he said, "because I'm still in charge of this operation, and whatever you may think of my actions, I still follow orders. You're required to be in attendance, and I want *that* in the report."

"It's noted, Commander."

He glanced at her quickly. There had been neither tone nor inflection revealing her hatred, but it trembled in the air between them.

"I expected something more from you."

She continued staring at the black, featureless cube in the middle of the plain. "Such as?"

"A comment. An assessment of military priorities. A plea to spare these cultural treasures. Something ... anything ... to justify your position."

She looked at him and saw the depth of distaste he held for her. Was it her *Amicus* status, or herself he feared and despised? Had she been repelled less by his warrior manner, she might have pitied him—"There are men whom one hates until that moment when one sees, through a chink in their armor, the sight of something nailed down and in torment."

"The validity of my position will ensure you never go to space again, Commander. If there were more I could do, something immediate and final, I would do it, by all the sweet dear souls in Hell. But I can't. You're in charge here, and the best I can do is record what I think insane behavior."

His anger flared again, and for a moment she thought he might hit her a second time, and she dropped back a step into a self-defense position. The first time he had taken her unaware; there would be no second time; she was capable of crippling him.

"Let me tell you a thing, *Amicus*, Friend of the Enemy! You follow that word all the way? The *Enemy*? You're a paid spy for the Enemy. An Enemy that's out to kill us, every one of us, that will stop nowhere short of total annihilation of the human race. The Kyben feed off a hatred of humankind unknown to any other race in the galaxy ..."

"My threshold for jingoism is very low, Commander. If you have some information to convey, do so. Otherwise, I'll return to Stand of Light."

He breathed deeply, damping his rage, and when he could speak again he said, "Whether this planet has what I think it has, or not, quite clearly it's been a prize for a long time. A *long* time. A lot longer than *either* of us can imagine. Long before the war moved into this sector. It's been conquered and reconquered and conquered all over again. The planet's *lousy* with every marauding race I've ever even *heard* of. The place is like Terran China ... let itself be overrun and probably didn't even put up a fight. Let the hordes in, submitted, and waited for them to be swallowed up. But more kept coming. There's something here they all wanted."

She had deduced as much herself; she needed no long-winded superficial lectures about the obvious. "And you think whatever it is they wanted is in the fifty forts. Have you spoken to any of the prisoners?"

"I've seen intelligence reports."

"But have you spoken to any of the prisoners *personally?*"

"Are you trying to make a case for incompetence, too?"

"All I asked is if you've spoken—"

"*No, dammit, I haven't spoken to any of that scum!*"

"Well, you should have!"

"To what end, Friend?" And he waved to his adjutant.

Drabix was in motion now. Lynn Ferraro could see there was nothing short of assassination that would stop him. And that was beyond her. "Because if you'd spoken to them, you'd have learned that whatever lives inside those forts has *permitted* the planet to be conquered. It doesn't care, as long as everyone minds their own business."

Drabix smiled, then snickered. "*Amicus*, go sit down somewhere, will you. The heat's getting to you."

"They say even the Kyben were tolerated, Commander. I'm warning you; let the forts alone."

"Fade off, Friend Ferraro. Command means decision, and my orders were to secure this planet. Secure doesn't mean fifty impregnable fortresses left untouched, and command doesn't mean letting bleeding hearts like you scare us into inaction with bogey men."

The adjutant stood waiting. "Mr. Lalwani," Drabix said, "tell the ground batteries to commence on signal. Concentrate fire on the southern face of that cube."

"Yes, sir." He went away quickly.

"It's war, Commander. That's your only answer, that it's war?"

Drabix would not look at her now. "That's right. It's a war to the finish. They declared it, and it's been that way for forty years. I'm doing my job ... and if that makes doing yours difficult, perhaps it'll show those pimply-assed bureaucrats at Central we need more ships and less Friends of the Enemy. *Something* has to break this stalemate with the Kyben, and even if I don't see the end of it I'll be satisfied knowing I was the one who broke it."

He gave the signal.

From concealed positions, lancet batteries opened up on the silent black cube on the plain.

Crackling beams of leashed energy erupted from the projectors, criss-crossed as they sped toward their target and impacted on the near face of the cube. Where they struck, novae of light appeared. Drabix lowered the visor on his battle helmet. "Protect your eyes, Friend," he warned.

Lynn dropped her visor, and heard herself shouting above the sudden crash of sound, "Let them alone!"

And in that instant she realized no one had asked the right question: where *were* the original natives of this world?

But it was too late to ask that question.

The barrage went on for a very long time.

Drabix was studying the southern face of the cube through a cyclop. The reports he had received were even more disturbing than the mere presence of the forts: the lancets had caused no visible damage.

Whatever formed those cubes, it was beyond the destructive capabilities of the ground batteries. The barrage had drained their power sources, and still the fort stood unscathed.

"Let them alone? Don't disturb them? *Now* do you see the danger, the necessity?" Drabix was spiraling upward, his frustration and anxiety making his voice brittle and high. "Tell me how we secure a war zone with the Enemy in our midst, Friend?"

"They aren't the Enemy!" she insisted.

"Leave them alone, eh?"

"They *want* to be left alone."

Drabix sneered at her, took one last look through the cyclop, and pulled the communicator loose from his wristcuff. He spoke directly to the *Descartes*, hanging in space above them. "Mr. Kokonen!"

The voice came back, clear and sharp. "Yes, sir?"

"On signal, pour everything you've got into the primary lancets. Hit it dead center. And keep it going till you open it up."

"On signal, sir."

"Drabix! Wait for Central to—"

"Minus three!"

"Let it alone! Let me try another—"

"Minus two!"

"Drabix ... stop ..."

"Minus one! Go to Hell, Friend!"

"You're out of your—"

"Commence firing!"

The lancet hurtled down out of the sky like a river of light. It struck the cube with a force that dwarfed the sum total of annihilation visited on the cube all that day. The sound rolled across the plain and the light was blinding. Explosions came so close together they merged into one endless report, the roof of the cube bathed in withering brilliance that rivaled the sun.

Lynn Ferraro heard herself screaming.

And suddenly, the lancet beam was cut off. Not from its source, but at its target. As though a giant, invisible hand had smothered the beam, it hurtled down out of the sky from the invisible dreadnought far above and ended in the sky above the cube. Then, as Drabix watched with eyes widening, and the *Amicus* watched with open terror choking her, the beam was snuffed out all

81

along its length. It disappeared back up its route of destructive force, into the sky, into the clouds, into the upper atmosphere and was gone.

A moment later, a new sun lit the sky as the dreadnought *Descartes* was strangled with its own weapon. It flared suddenly, blossomed ... and was gone.

Then the cube began to rise from the earth. However much larger it was than what was revealed on the plain, Lynn Ferraro could not begin to estimate. It rose up and up, now no longer a squat cube, becoming a terrifying pillar of featureless black that dominated the sky. Somehow, she knew at forty-nine other locations around the planet the remaining forts were also rising.

After endless centuries of solitude, whatever lived in those structures was awakening at last.

They had been content to let the races of the galaxy come and go and conquer and be assimilated, as long as they were not severely threatened. They might have allowed humankind to come here and exist, or they might have allowed the Kyben the same freedom. But not both.

Drabix was whimpering beside her.

And not even her pity for him could save them.

He looked at her, white-eyed. "You got your wish," she said. "The war is over."

The original natives of the planet were taking a hand, at last. The stalemate was broken. A third force had entered the war. And whether they would be inimical to Terrans or Kyben, no one could know. *Amicus* Ferraro grew cold as the cube rose up out of the plain, towering above everything.

It was clear: roused from sleep, the inhabitants of the fifty forts would never consider themselves Friends of the Enemy.

"How did you come to write this story?" I am frequently asked, whether it be this story, or that one over there, or the soft pink-and-white one in the corner. Usually, I shrug helplessly. My ideas come from the same places yours come from: Compulsion City, about half an hour out of Schenectady. I can't give a more specific location than that. Once in a great while, I know specifically. The story that follows is one of those instances, and I will tell you. I attended the 22nd World Science Fiction Convention (Pacificon II) on Labor Day, 1964. For the past many "cons," a feature has been a fan-art exhibit, with artwork entered by nonprofessionals from all over the science fiction world. Several times (for some as-yet-unexplained reason) I have been asked to be among the judges of this show, and have found the level of work to be pleasantly high, in some cases really remarkable. On half a dozen occasions I have found myself wondering why the certain illustrator that impressed me was not working deep in the professional scene; and within a year, invariably, that artist has left the amateur ranks and become a selling illustrator. At the Pacificon, once again I attended the fan-art exhibition. I was in the company of Robert Silverberg, a writer whose name will not be unfamiliar to you, and the then-editor of Amazing Stories, *Cele Goldsmith Lalli (the Lalli had only recently been added, when that handsome bachelor lady finally threw in the sponge and married Mr. Lalli, in whose direction dirty looks for absconding with one of the ablest editors s-f had yet produced). Cele had been trying vainly to get a story out of me. I was playing coy. There had*

been days when the cent or cent-and-a-half Amazing Stories *paid was* mucho dinero *to me, but now I was a Big-Time Hollywood Writer (it says here somewhere) and I was enjoying saying stupid things like, "You can't afford me, Cele," or "I'll see if Joseph E. Levine will let me take off a week to write one for you ... I'll have my agent call you." Cele was taking it staunchly. Since I was much younger, and periodically disrupted her efficient Ziff-Davis office, she had tolerated me with a stoic resign only faintly approached by the Colossus of Rhodes. "Okay, okay, big shot," she was replying, "I'll stretch it to two cents a word, and we both know you're being overpaid." I sneered and marched away. It was something of a running gunbattle for two days. But, in point of fact, I was so tied up with prior commitments in television (that was my term of menial servitude on "The Outer Limits") that I knew I didn't have the time for short stories, much as I lusted to do a few, to keep my hand in. That Sunday morning in September, we were at the fan-art exhibit, and I was stopped in front of a display of scratchboard illustrations by a young man named Dennis Smith, from Chula Vista, California. They were extraordinary efforts, combining the best features of Finlay, Lawrence, and Heinrich Kley. They were youthfully derivative, of course, but professionally executed, and one of them held me utterly fascinated. It was a scene on a foggy landscape, with a milk-wash of stars dripping down the sky, a dim outline of battlements in the distance, and in the foreground, a weird phosphorescent creature with great luminous eyes, holding a bag of skulls, astride a giant rat, padding toward me. I stared at it for a long while, and a small group of people clustered behind me, also held by the picture. "If somebody would buy that, I'd write the story for it," I heard myself say. And from behind me, Cele Goldsmith Lalli's margarine-warm voice replied, "I'll buy it for* Fantastic; *you've got an assignment." I was trapped. Hell hath no fury like the wrath of an editor with single-minded devotion to duty. Around that strange, remarkable drawing, I wrote a story, one of my personal favorites. Dennis Smith had named the picture, so I felt it only seemly to title the story the same:*

Bright Eyes

F eet without toes. Softly-padded feet, furred. Footsteps sounded gently, padding furry, down ink-chill corridors of the place. A place Bright Eyes had inhabited since before time had substance. Since before places had names. A dark place, a shadowed place, only a blot against the eternally nightened skies. No stars chip-ice twittered insanely against that night; for in truth the night was mad enough.

Night was a condition Bright Eyes understood. And he knew about day ... He knew about almost everything.

The worms. The moles. The trunks of dead trees. The whites of eggs. Music. And random sounds. The sound fish make in the deep. The flares of the sun. The scratch of unbleached cloth against flesh. The hounds that roamed the tundra. The way those who have hair see it go pale and stiff with age. Clocks and what they do. Ice cream. Wax seals on parchment dedications. Grass and leaves. Metal and wood. Up and down. Here and most of there. Bright Eyes knew it all.

And that was the reason his padding, acoustically-sussurating footsteps hissed high in the dark, beamed, silent corridors of the place. And why he would now, forever at last, make that long journey.

The giant rat, whose name was Thomas, lay curled, fetid, sleeping, near the great wooden gate; and as Bright Eyes approached, it stirred. Then, like a mastiff, it lifted its bullet-shaped head, and the bright crimson eyes flickered artful awareness. The massive head stiffened on the neckless neck, and it shambled to its feet. The wire tail swished across hand-inset cobblestones, making scratching sounds in the silent night.

"It's time," Bright Eyes murmured. "Here, Thomas." The great grey creature jogged to him, nuzzling Bright Eyes' leg. It sniffed at the net filled with old skulls, and its whiskers twitched like cilia for a moment.

Bright Eyes swung the great wooden gate open with difficulty, dislodging caked dirt and cold-hardened clots of stray matter. The heavy metal ring clanged as he dropped it against the portal. Then Bright Eyes swung to the back of the rat, and without reins or prompting, the rat whose name was Thomas, paced steadily through the opening, leaving behind the only home Bright Eyes had ever known, which he would never see again. There was mist on the land.

Strange and terrible portents had caused Bright Eyes to leave the place. Unwilling to believe what they implied, at first, Bright Eyes pursued the gentle patterns of his days—like all the other days he had ever known, alone. But finally, when the blood-red and grey colors washed in unholy mixture down the skies, he knew what had happened, and that it was his obligation to return to a place he had never seen, had only heard about from others, centuries before, and do what had to be done. The others were long-since dead: had been dead since before Christ took Barabbas's place on the cross. The place to which Bright Eyes must return had not even been known, had not even existed, when the others left the world. Yet it was Bright Eyes' place, by default, and his obligation to all the others who had passed before. Since he was the last of his kind, a race that had no name, and had dwelled in the castle-place for millennia, he only dimly understood what was demanded of him. Yet this he knew: the call had been made, the portents cast into the night to be seen by him; and he must go.

It was a journey whose length even Bright Eyes could not surmise. The mist seemed to cover the world in a soft shroud that promised little good luck on this mission.

And, inexplicably, to Bright Eyes, there was a crushing sadness in him. A sadness he did not fathom, could not plumb, dared not examine. His glowing sight pierced through the mist as, steadily and stately, Thomas moved toward Bright Eyes' final destination. And it would remain unknown, till he reached it.

Out of the mist the giant rat swung jauntily. They had passed among softly-rounded hills with water that dropped from above. Then the shoulders had become black rock, and gleaming pinpoints of diamond brilliance had shone

86

in the rock, and Bright Eyes had realized they were in caves. But had they come from the land, inside ... or had they come from some resting-land deep in the bowels of the Earth, into these less hidden caverns; and would they continue to another outside?

Far ahead, a dim light pulsed and glowed, and Bright Eyes spurred Thomas forward. The dim light grew more bold, more orange and yellow and menacing with sudden soft roars of bubbling thunder. And as they rounded the passage, the floor of the cave was gone, and in their path lay a boiling scar in the stone. A lava pit torn up out of the solid stone, hissing and bubbling fiercely with demonic abandon. The light burned at Bright Eyes, and the heat was gagging. The sour stench of sulphur bit at his senses, and he made to turn aside.

The giant rat suddenly bolted in panic, arching back, more like caterpillar than rodent, and Bright Eyes was tossed to the floor of the cave, his net of skulls rolling away from him. Thomas chittered in fear, and took steps away, then paused and returned to his master. Bright Eyes rose and patted the terrified beast several times. Thomas fell into quivering silence.

Bright Eyes retrieved the skulls. All but one, that had rolled across the stone floor and disappeared with a vagrant hiss into the flame-pit. The giant rat sniffed at the walls, first one, then the other, and settled against the far one. Bright Eyes contemplated the gash in the stone floor. It stretched completely across, and as far as he could tell, forward. Thomas chittered.

Bright Eyes looked away from the flames, into the fear-streaked eyes of the beast. "Well, Thomas?" he asked. The rat's snout twitched, and it hunkered closer to the wall. It looked up at Bright Eyes imploringly. Bright Eyes came to the rat, crouched down, stroked its neat, tight fur. Bright Eyes brushed the wall. It was not hot. It was cool.

The rat knew.

Bright Eyes rose, walked back along the passage. He found the parallel corridor half a mile back in the direction they had come. Without turning, he knew Thomas had silently followed, and leading the way, he moved down the parallel corridor, in coolness. Even the Earth could not keep Bright Eyes from what had to be done.

They followed the corridor for a very long time, till the rock walls leaned inward, and the littered floor tilted toward the stalactite-spiked ceiling. Bright Eyes dismounted, and walked beside the giant rat. There were strange, soft murmurings beneath them. Thomas chittered every time the Earth rattled. Further on, the passage puckered narrower and narrower ... and Bright Eyes was forced to bend, then stoop, then crawl. Thomas slithered belly-tight behind him, more frightened to be left behind than to struggle forward.

A whisper of chill, clean air passed them.

They moved ahead, only the glow of Bright Eyes marking a passage.

87

Abruptly, the cave mouth opened onto darkness, and cold, and the world Bright Eyes had never seen, the world his dim ancestors had left millennia before.

No one could ever set down what that first sight meant to Bright Eyes. But ... the chill he felt was not the chill of the night wind.

The countryside was a murmuring silence. The sky was so black, not even the stars seemed at home. Frightened, lonely, and alienated from the universe they populated, the silver specks drifted down the night like chalk dust. And through the strangeness, Bright Eyes rode Thomas, neither seeing nor caring. Behind him a village passed over the horizon line, and he never knew he had been through it.

No shouts of halt were hurled on the wind. No one came to darkened windows to see Bright Eyes pass through. He was approaching there and gone, all in an instant of time that may have been forever and may have been never. He was a wraith on the mist-bottomed silence. And Thomas moved stately through valley and village, only paced, nothing more. From now on, it was Bright Eyes' problem.

Far out on the plains, the wind opened up suddenly. It spun down out of the northwest and drove at Bright Eyes' back. And on the trembling coolness, the alien sounds of wild dogs came snapping across the emptiness. Bright Eyes looked up, and Thomas's neck-hair bristled with fear. Bright Eyes stroked a round, palpitating ear and the great rat came under control.

Then, almost without sound that was tied to them—for the sound of dogs came from a distance, from far away—the insane beasts were upon them. A slavering band of crimson-eyed mongrels, some still wearing dog collars and clinking tags, hair grown shaggy and matted with filth. Noses with large nostrils, as though they had had to learn to forage the land all at once, rather than from birth. These were the dogs of the people, driven out onto the wind, to live or die or eat each other as best they could.

The first few leaped from ten feet away, high and flat in trajectories that brought them down on Thomas's back, almost into Bright Eyes' lap, their yellow teeth scraping and clattering like dice on cement, lunacy bubbling out of them as froth and stench and spastic claw-scrabblings. Thomas reared and Bright Eyes slid off without losing balance, using the bag of skulls as a mace to ward off the first of the vicious assaults. One great Doberman had its teeth set for a strike into Thomas's belly, but the great rat—with incredible ferocity and skill—snapped it head down in a scythelike movement, and rent the greybrown beast from jowl to chest, and it fell away, bleeding, moaning piteously.

And the rest of the pack materialized from the darkness. Dozens of them, circling warily now that one of their number lay in a trembling-wet garbage heap of its own innards.

Bright Eyes whistled Thomas to him with a soft sound. They stood together, facing the horde, and Bright Eyes called up a talent his race had not been forced to use in uncounted centuries.

The great white eyes glowed, deep and bubbling as cauldrons of lava, and a hollow moaning came from a place deep in Bright Eyes' throat. A sound of torment, a sound of fear, an evocation of gods that were dust before the Earth began to gather moisture to itself in the senseless cosmos, before the Moon had cooled, before the patterns of magnetism had settled the planets of the Solar System in their sockets.

Out of that sound, the basic fiber of emotion, like some great machine phasing toward top-point efficiency, Bright Eyes drew himself tight and unleashed the blast of pure power at the dogs.

Buried deep in his mind, the key to pure fear as a weapon was depressed, and in a blinding fan of sweeping brilliance, the emotion washed out toward the horde, a comber of undiluted, unbuffered terror. For the first time in centuries, that immense power was unleashed. Bright Eyes *thought* them terrified, and the air stank with fear.

The dogs, bulge-eyed and hysterical, fled in a wave of yipping, trembling, tuck-tailed quivering.

As if the night could no longer contain the immensity of it, the shimmering sound of terror bulged and grew, seeking release in perhaps another dimension, some higher threshold of audibility, and finding none—it wisped away in darkness and was gone.

Bright Eyes stood trembling uncontrollably, every fiber of his body spasming. His pineal gland throbbed. An intracranial tumor—whose presence in a human brain would have meant death—absolutely imperative for Bright Eyes' coordinated thought processes, which had swollen to five times its size as he concentrated, till his left temple had bulged with the pressing growth of it ... now shrank, subsided, sucked itself back down into the grey brain matter, the gliomas itself. And slowly, as the banked fires of his eyes softened once more, Bright Eyes came back to full possession of himself.

"It has been a very long time since that was needed," he said gently, and dwelt for a moment on the powers his race had possessed, powers long since gone to forgetfulness.

Now that it was over, the giant rat settled to the ground, licking at its fur, at a slash in the flesh where one of the mad things had ripped and found meat.

Bright Eyes went to him. "They are the saddest creatures of all. They are alone." Thomas continued licking at his wounds.

Days later, but closer to their final destination, they came to the edge of a great river. At one time it had been a swiftly moving stream, whipping itself high in a pounding torrent filled with colors and sounds; but now it flushed itself to the sea wearily, riding low in its own tide-trough, and hampered by the logjam. The logjam was made of corpses.

Bodies, hideously bloated and maggot-white puffed out of human shapes, lay across one another, from the near shore to the opposite bank. Thousands of bodies, uncountable thousands, twisted and piled and washed together till it would have been possible to cross the river on the top layer of naked men's faces, bleached women's backs, twisted children's hands crinkled as if left too long in water. For they had been.

As far upstream as Bright Eyes could see, and as far downstream as the bend of the banks permitted, it was the same. No movement, save the very seldom jiggle of a corpse as the water passed through. For they were packed so deep and so tight, that in truth only water at its most sluggish could wanly press through. Yet the water gurgled and twittered among them, stealing slowly downstream—caressing rotting flesh in obscene parody: water, cleansing stepping-stones; polishing and smoothing and drenching them senselessly as it marks its passage only by what is left behind.

That was the ultimate horror of this river of dead: that the tide—no matter how held-back now—continued unheeding as it had since the world was born. For the world went on. And did not care.

Bright Eyes stood silently. At the bottom of the short slope that ended with shoreline, bodies were strewn in a jackstraw tumble. He breathed very deeply, fighting for air, and the shivering started again. As it grew more pronounced, there was a movement in the dry-moist river bed. Bodies abruptly began to move. They trembled as though roiling in a stream growing turbulent. Then, one by one, they rearranged themselves. All up and down the length of the river, the bodies shifted and moved and lifted without aid from their original positions, and far off, where their movement to neatness could not be seen, there came the roar of dammed-up water breaking free, surging forward, freed from its restraining walls of once-human flesh.

As Bright Eyes trembled, power surging through his slight frame, his eyes seeming to wax and wane with currents of electricity, the river of corpses freed itself from its logjam, and was open once more.

The water poured in a great frothing wave down and down the corpse-bordered trough of the river. It broke out of a box-canyon to Bright Eyes' left, like a wild creature penned too long and at last set free on the wind. It came bubbling, boiling, threshing forward, passed the spot where he stood, and hurled itself away around the bend in the shoreline.

As Bright Eyes felt the trembling pass, the river rose, and rose, and gently now, rose. Covering the ghastly residue of humanity that now lay submerged beneath the mud-blackened waters.

The eyes of the trembling creature, the eyes of the giant rat, the eyes of the uncaring day were blessedly relieved of the sight of decay and death.

Emotions washed quickly, one after another, down his features; washed as quickly as the river had concealed its sad wealth; colors of sadness, imprinted in a manner no human being could ever have conceived, for the face that supported these emotions was of a race that had vanished before man had walked the Earth.

Then Bright Eyes turned, and with the rat, walked upstream. Toward the morning.

When the bleeding birds went over, the sun darkened. Great irregular, hard-edged clouds of them, all species, all wingspreads—but silent. Passing across the broad, grey brow of the sky, heading absolutely nowhere, they turned off the sun. It was suddenly chill as a crypt. Heading East. Not toward warmth, or instinct, or destination ... just anywhere, nowhere. Until they wearied, expired, dropped. Not manna, garbage. Live garbage that fell in hundred-clots from the beat-winged flights.

Many dropped, fluttering idly as if too weary to fight the air currents any longer. As though what tiny instinctual brain substance they had possessed, was now baked, turned to jelly, squashed by an unnameable force into an ichorous juice that ran out through their eyes. As though they no longer cared to live, much less to continue this senseless flight East to nowhere ...

... and they bled.

A rain of bird's blood, sick and discolored. It misted down, beading Bright Eyes, and the stiff rat fur, and the trees, and the still, silent, dark land.

Only the dead, flat no-sound of millions of wings metronomically beating, beating, beating ...

Bright Eyes shuddered, turned his face from the sight above, and finding himself unable to look yet unable to end the horror as he had the mad dogs or the water of corpses, sought surcease in his own personal vision.

And this, which had driven him forth, was his vision:

Sleeping, deep in that place where he had lived so long, Bright Eyes had felt the subtle altering of tempo in the air around him. It was nothing as obvious as machinery beginning to whirr, trembling the walls around him; nor as complex as a shift in dimensional orientation. It was, rather, a soft sliding in the molecules of everything except Bright Eyes. For an instant everything went just slightly out of synch, a little fuzzy, and Bright Eyes came awake sharply. The *thing* that had occurred, was something his race had preset aeons before. It was triggered to activate itself—whatever "itself" was—after certain events had *possibly* happened.

91

The fact that this shifting had occurred, made Bright Eyes grow cold and wary. He had expected to die without its ever having come. But now, this was the time, and it *had* happened, and he waited for the next phase.

It came quickly. The vision.

The air before him grew even more indistinct, more roiled, like a pool of quicksilver smoke tumbling in and in on itself. And from that cloudiness the image of the last of the Castellans took shape. (Was it image, or reality, or thought within his head? He did not really know, for Bright Eyes was merely the last of his kind, no specially trained adept, and much of what his race had been, and knew, was lost to him, beyond him.)

The Castellan was a fifth-degree adept, and surely the last remaining one of Bright Eyes' race to—go. He wore the purple and blue of royalty, from a House Bright Eyes did not recognize, but the cut of the robe was shorter than styles Bright Eyes recalled as having been current—then. And the Castellan's cowl was up, revealing a face that was bleak with sorrow and even a hint of cruelty. Such was not present, of course, for the Castellans merely performed their duties, but Bright Eyes was certain *this* adept had been against the decision to—go. Yet he had been chosen to bring the message to Bright Eyes.

He stood, booted and silent, in the soft-washed blue and white lightness of Bright Eyes' sleeping chamber. Bright Eyes was given time to come to full wakefulness, and then the Castellan spoke.

"What you see has been gone for ten centuries. I am the last, save you. They have set me the task, and this twist of my being, of telling you what you must do. If the proper portents trigger my twist to appear before you—pray it never happens—than you must go to the city of the ones with hair, the ones who come after us, the ones who inherit the Earth, the men. Go to their city, with a bag of skulls of our race. You will know what to do with them.

"Know this, Bright Eyes: we go voluntarily. Some of us—and I am one of them—more reluctantly than most. It is a decision that seems only proper. Those who come after us, Men, will have their chance for the stars. This was the only gift of birth we could offer. No other gift can have meaning between us. They must have our chance, so we have gone to the place where you now lie. By the time I appear to you—if ever I do—we will be gone. This is the way of it, a sad and inescapable way. You will be the last. And now I will show you a thing."

The Castellan raised his hands before his face, and as though they were growing transparent, they glowed with an inner fire. The Visioning power. The Castellan's face suffused with flames as it conjured up the proper vision for Bright Eyes.

It appeared out of lines of blossoming crimson force, in the very air beside the Castellan. A vision of terror and destruction. Flames man-made and devastating, incredible in their hell-fire. Like some great arachnid of pure force, the demon flames of the destruction swept and washed across the vision, and when it faded, Bright Eyes lay shaken by what he had seen.

"If this that I have shown you ever comes to pass, then my twist will appear to you. And if you ever hear me as you hear me now, then go, with the bag of skulls of our people. And do not doubt your feelings.

"For if I appear to you, it will all have been in vain, and those of us who were less pure in our motivations, will have been proved right."

Shimmering substance, coalescing nothingness, air that trembled and twittered in re-forming, and the Castellan was gone. Bright Eyes rose, and gathered the skulls from the crypt. Then:

Feet without toes. Softly-padded feet, furred. Footsteps sounded gently, padding furry, down ink-chill corridors of the place. A place Bright Eyes had inhabited since before time had substance. He walked through night, out of the place.

Night was a condition Bright Eyes understood. And he knew about day ...

The bleeding birds were long since gone. Bright Eyes moved through the days, and onward. At one point he passed through a sector of trembling mountains, that heaved up great slabs of rock and hurled them away like epileptics ridding themselves of clothes. The ground trembled and burst and screamed and the very Earth went insane to tunes of destruction it had never written.

There was a plain of dead grass, sere and wasted with great heaps of desic-cated insects heaped here, there. They had flocked together to the last resting place, and the plain of dead grass was poor tapestry indeed to hold the impris-oned pigments of their dead flesh, the acrid and bitter-sweet pervasive odor of formic acid that lingered like hot breath of a mad giant across the silent windless emptiness. Yet, how faint, a sound of weeping ...?

Finally, Bright Eyes came to the city.

Thomas would not enter. The twisted rope-pillars of smoke that still climbed relentlessly to the dark sky; the terrible sounds of steel cracking and masonry falling into empty streets; the charnel-house odor. Thomas would not go in.

But Bright Eyes was compelled to enter. Into that last debacle of all. From where it had begun.

The dead were everywhere, sighing soundlessly with milk-white eyes at a tomorrow that had never come. And each fallen one soundlessly spoke the question of why. Bright Eyes walked with the burden of chaos pulsing in him. This is what it had come to.

For this, his race had gone away. That the ones with hair, the men they had been called, they had called themselves, could stride the Earth. How

93

cheap they had left it all. How cheap, how thin, how sordid. This was the last of it, the last of the race of men. Dust and dead.

Down a street, women pleading out of death for mercy.

Through what had been a park, old men humped crazily in rigorous failure to escape.

Past a structure, building front ripped away as if fingernails had shorn it clean. Children's arms, pocked and burned, dangling. Tiny hands.

To another place. Not like the place from which Bright Eyes had come, but the place to which he had journeyed. No special marker, just ... a place. Sufficient.

And then it was, that Bright Eyes sank to his knees, crying. Tears that had not been seen since before Man had come from caves, tears that Bright Eyes had never known. Infinite sadness. Cried. Cried for the ghosts of the creatures with hair, cried for Men. For Man. Each Man. The Man who had done away with himself so absurdly, so completely. Bright Eyes, on his knees, sorrowing for the ones who had lived here, and were gone, leaving him to the night, and the silence, and eternity. A melody never to be heard again.

He placed the skulls. Down in the soft white ash. Unresponsive, dying Earth, receiving its burden testament.

Bright Eyes, last of a race that had condemned itself to extinction, had condemned *him* to living in darkness forever, and had had only the saving wistful knowledge that the race coming after would live in the world. But now, gone, all of them, taking the world with them, leaving instead—no fair exchange—charnel house.

And Bright Eyes; alone.

Not only *their* race had been destroyed, in vain, but *his*, centuries turned to mud and diamonds in their markerless graves, had passed in futility. It had all, all of it, been for nothing.

So Bright Eyes—never Man—was the last man on Earth. Keeper of a silent graveyard; echoless tomb monument to the foolishness, the absurdity, of nobility.

Pretty people have it easier than uglies. It smacks of cliché, and yet the lovelies of this world, defensive to the grave, will say, 'tain't so. They will contend that nice makes it harder for them. They get hustled more, people try to use them more, and to hear girls tell it, their good looks are nothing but curse, curse, curse. But stop to think: at least a good-looking human being has that much going for openers. Plain to not-so-nice-at-all folk have to really jump for every little crumb. Things come harder to them. The reasoning of the rationale is a simple one: we worship the Pepsi Generation. We have a pathological lemming drive to conceal our age, lift our faces, dress like overblown Shirley Temples, black that grey in the hair, live a lie. What ever happened to growing old gracefully, the reverence of maturity, the search for character as differentiated from superficial comeliness? It be a disease, I warn you. It will rot you from the inside, while the outside glows. It will escalate into a culture that can never tolerate

The Discarded

Bedzyk saw Riila go mad, and watched her throw herself against the Lucite port, till her pinhead was a red blotch of pulped flesh and blood. He sighed, and sucked deeply from his massive bellows chest, and wondered how he, of all the Discards, had been silently nominated the leader. The ship hung in space, between the Moon and Earth, unwanted, unnoticed, a raft adrift in the sea of night.

Around him in the ship's saloon, the others watched Riila killing herself, and when her body fell to the rug, they turned away, allowing Bedzyk his choice of who was to dispose of her. He chose John Smith—the one with feathers where hair should have been—and the nameless one who clanged instead of talking.

The two of them lifted her heavy body, with its tiny pea of head, and carried it to the garbage port. They emptied it, opened it, tossed her inside, redogged, and blew her out. She floated past the saloon window on her way sunward. In a moment she was lost.

Bedzyk sat down in a deep chair and drew breath whistlingly into his mighty chest. It was a chore, being leader of these people.

People? No, that was certainly not the word. These Discards. That was a fine willowy word to use. They were scrap, refuse, waste, garbage themselves.

How fitting for Riila to have gone that way, out the garbage port. They would *all* bid good-bye that way some day. He noted there was no 'day' on the ship. But some good *something*—maybe day, maybe night—each of them would go sucking out that port like the garbage.

It had to be that way. They were Discards.

But people? No, they were not people. People did not have hooks where hands should have been, nor one eye, nor carapaces, nor humps on chests and backs, nor fins, nor any of the other mutations these residents of the ship sported. People were normal. Evenly matched sets of arms and legs and eyes. Evenly matched husbands, wives. Evenly distributed throughout the Solar System, and evenly dividing the goods of the System between themselves and the frontier worlds at the Edge. And all happily disposed to let the obscene Discards die in their prison ship.

"She's gone."

He had pursed his lips, had sunk his perfectly normal head onto his gigantic chest, and had been thinking. Now he looked up at the speaker. It was John Smith, with feathers where hair should have been.

"I said: she's gone."

Bedzyk nodded without replying. Riila had been just one more in the tradition. They had already lost over two hundred Discards from the ship. There would be more.

Strange how these—he hesitated again to use the word *people*, finally settled on the word they used among themselves: creatures—these *creatures* had steeled themselves to the death of one of their kind. Or perhaps they did not consider the rest as malformed as themselves. Each person on the ship was different. No two had been affected by the Sickness in the same way. The very fibers of the muscles had altered with some of these creatures, making their limbs useless; on others the pores had clogged on their skin surfaces, eliminating all hair. On still others strange juices had been secreted in the blood stream, causing weird growths to erupt where smoothness had been. But perhaps each one thought he was less hideous than the others. It was conceivable. Bedzyk knew his great chest was not nearly as unpleasant to look upon as, say, Samswope's spiny crest and twin heads. *In fact, Bedzyk mused wryly, many people might think it was becoming, this great wedge of a chest, all matted with dark hair and heroic-seeming. Uh-huh, the others are pretty miserable to look at, but not me, especially.* Yes, it was conceivable.

In any case, they paid no attention now, if one of their group killed himself. They turned away; most of them were better off dead, anyhow.

Then he caught himself.

He was starting to get like the rest of them! He had to stop thinking like that. It wasn't right. No one should be allowed to take death like that.

He resolved, the next one would be stopped, and he would deliver them a stern warning, and tell the Discards that they would find landfall soon, and to buck up.

But he knew he would sit and watch the next time, as he had this time. For he had made the same resolve before Riila had gone.

Samswope came into the saloon—he had been on KP all 'day' and both his heads were dripping with sweat—and picked his way among the conversing groups of Discards to the seat beside Bedzyk.

"Mmm." It was a greeting; he was identifying his arrival.

"Hi, Sam. How was it?"

"Metsoo-metz," he gibed, imitating Scalomina (the one-eyed ex-plumber, of Sicilian descent), tipping his hand in an obvious Scalominian gesture. "I'll live. Unfortunately." He added the last word with only a little drop of humor.

"Did I ever tell you the one about the Candy-Ass Canadian Boil-Sucker?" He didn't even smile as he said it; with either head. Bedzyk nodded wearily: he didn't want to play that game. "Yeah, well," Samswope said wearily. He sat silently for several long moments, then added, with irony, "But did I tell you I was married to her?" His wife had turned him in.

Morbidity ran knee-deep on the ship.

"Riila killed herself a little bit ago," Bedzyk said carelessly. There was no other way to say it.

"I figured as much," Samswope explained. "I saw them carrying her past the galley to the garbage lock. That's number six this week alone. You going to do anything, Bedzyk?"

Bedzyk twisted abruptly in his chair. He leveled a gaze at a spot directly between Samswope's two heads. His words were bitter with helplessness and anger that the burden should be placed upon him. "What do you mean, what am *I* going to do? I'm a prisoner here, too. When they had the big roundup, I got snatched away from a wife and three kids, the same as you got pulled away from your used car lot. What the hell do you want me to do? Beg them not to bash their heads against the Lucite, it'll smear our nice north view of space?"

Samswope wiped both hands across his faces simultaneously in a weary pattern. The blue eyes of his left head closed, and the brown eyes of his right head blinked quickly. His left head, which had been speaking till now, nodded onto his chest. His right head, the nearly-dumb one, mumbled incoherently—Samswope's left head jerked up, and a look of disgust and hatred clouded his eyes. "Shut up, you—fucking moron!" He cracked his right head with a full fist.

Bedzyk watched without pity. The first time he had seen Samswope flail himself—would flagellate be a better term?—he had pitied the mutant. But it was a constant thing now, the way Samswope took his agony out on the dumb head. And there were times Bedzyk thought Samswope was better off than most. At least he had a release valve, an object of hate.

"Take it easy, Sam. Nothing's going to help us, not a single, lousy th—"

Samswope snapped a look at Bedzyk, then catalogued the thick arms and huge chest of the man, and wearily murmured: "Oh, I don't know, Bedzyk, I don't know." He dropped his left head into his hands. The right one winked at Bedzyk with the archness of an imbecile. Bedzyk shuddered and looked away.

"If only we could have made that landing on Venus," Samswope intoned from the depths of his hands. "If only they'd let us in."

"You ought to know by now, Sam," Bedzyk reminded him bitterly, "there's no room for us in the System at all. No room on Earth and nowhere else. They've got allocations and quotas and assignments. So many to Io, so many to Callisto, so many to Luna and Venus and Mars and anyplace else you might want to settle down. No room for Discards. No room in space, at all."

Across the saloon three fish-men, their heads encased in bubbling clear helmets, had gotten into a squabble, and two of them were trying to open the petcock on the third's helmet. This was something else again; the third fish-man was struggling, he didn't want to die gasping. This was not a suicide, but a murder, if they let it go unchecked.

Bedzyk leaped to his feet and hurled himself at the two attacking fish-men. He caught one by the bicep and spun him. His fist was half-cocked before he realized one solid blow would shatter the water-globe surrounding the fish-face, would kill the mutant. Instead, he took him around and shoved him solidly by the back of the shoulders, toward the compartment door. The fish-man stumbled away, breathing bubbly imprecations into his life water, casting furious glances back at his companions. The second fish-man came away of his own accord and followed the first from the saloon.

Bedzyk helped the last fish-man to a relaxer and watched disinterestedly as the mutant let a fresh supply of air bubbles into the circulating water in the globe. The fish-man mouthed a lipless thanks, and Bedzyk passed it away with a gesture. He went back to his seat.

Samswope was massaging the dumb head. "Those three'll never grow up."

Bedzyk fell into the chair. "You wouldn't be too happy living inside a gold-fish bowl yourself, Swope."

Samswope stopped massaging the wrinkled yellow skin of the dumb head, seemed prepared to snap a retort, but a blip and clear-squawk from the intercom stopped him.

"Bedzyk! Bedzyk, you down there?" It was the voice of Harmony Teat up in the drive room. Why was it they always called *him*? Why did they persist in making him their arbiter?

"Yeah, I'm here, in the saloon. What's up?"

The squawk-box blipped again and Harmony Teat's mellow voice came to him from the ceiling. "I just registered a ship coming in on us, off about three-thirty. I checked through the ephemeris and the shipping schedules. Nothing supposed to be out there. What should I do? You think it's a customs ship from Earth?"

Bedzyk heaved himself to his feet. He sighed. "No, I don't think it's a customs ship. They threw us out, but I doubt if they have the imagination or gall to extract tithe from us for being here. I don't know what it might be, Harmony. Hold everything and record any signals they send. I'm on my way upship."

He strode quickly out of the saloon, and up the cross-leveled ramps toward the drive room. Not till he had passed the hydroponics level did he realize Samswope was behind him. "I, uh, thought I'd come along, Bed," Samswope said apologetically, wringing his small, red hands. "I didn't want to stay down there with those—those freaks."

His dumb head hung off to one side, sleeping fitfully.

Bedzyk did not answer. He turned on his heel and casually strode updecks, not looking back.

There was no trouble. The ship identified itself when it was well away. It was an Attaché Carrier from System Central in Butte, Montana, Earth. The supercargo was a SpecAttaché named Curran. When the ship pulled along-side the Discard vessel and jockeyed for grappling position, Harmony Teat (her long grey-green hair reaching down past the spiked projections on her spinal column) threw on the *attract* field for that section of the hull. The Earth ship clunked against the Discard vessel, and the locks were synched in.

Curran came across without a suit.

He was a slim, incredibly tanned young man with a crew cut clipped so short a patch of nearly-bald showed at the center of his scalp. His eyes were alert and his manner was brisk and friendly, that of the professional dignitary in the Foreign Service.

Bedzyk did not bother with amenities.

"What do you want?"

"Who may I be addressing, sir, if I may ask?" Curran was the perfect model of diplomacy.

"Bedzyk is what I was called on Earth." Cool, disdainful, I-may-be-hideous-but-I-still-have-a-little-pride.

"My name is Curran, Mr. Curran, Mr. Bedzyk. Alan Curran of System Central. I've been asked to come out and speak to you about—"

Bedzyk settled against the bulkhead opposite the lock, not even offering the attaché an invitation to return to the saloon.

100

"You want us to get out of your sky, is that it? You stinking lousy ..." He faltered in fury. He could not finish the sentence, so steeped in anger was he. "You set off too many bombs down there, and eventually some of us with something in our bloodstreams react to it, and we turn into monsters. What do you do ... you call it the Sickness and you pack us up whether we want to go or not, and you shove us into space."

"Mr. Bedzyk, I—"

"You *what?* You damned well *what*, Mr. System Central? With your straight, clean body and your nice home on Earth, and your allocations of how many people live where, to keep the balance of culture just so! You *what?* You want to invite us to leave? Okay, we'll go!" He was nearly screeching, his face crimson with emotion, his big hands knotted at his sides for fear he would strike this emissary.

"We'll get out of your sky. We've been all the way out to the Edge, Mr. Curran, and there's no room in space for us anywhere. They won't let us land even on the frontier worlds where we can pay our way. Oh no; contamination, they think. Okay, don't shove, Curran, we'll be going."

He started to turn away, was nearly down the passageway, when Curran's solid voice stopped him: "Bedzyk!"

The wedge-chested man turned. Curran was unsticking the seam that sealed his jumper top. He pulled it open and revealed his chest.

It was covered with leprous green and brown sores. His face was a blasted thing, then. He was a man with Sickness, who wanted to know how he had acquired it—how he could be rid of it. On the ship, they called Curran's particular deformity "the runnies."

Bedzyk walked back slowly, his eyes never leaving Curran's face. "They sent you to talk to us?" Bedzyk asked, wondering.

Curran resealed the jumper, and nodded. He laid a hand on his chest, as though wishing to be certain the sores would not run off and leave him. Terror swam brightly in his young eyes.

"It's getting worse down there, Bedzyk," he said as if in a terrible need for hurrying. "There are more and more changing every day. I've never seen anything like it—"

He hesitated, shuddered.

He ran a hand over his face, and swayed slightly, as though whatever memory he now clutched to himself was about to make him faint. "I—I'd like to sit down."

Bedzyk took him by the elbow, and led him a few steps toward the saloon. Then Dresden, the girl with the glass hands—who wore monstrous cotton-filled gloves—came out from the connecting passage leading to the saloon, and Bedzyk thought of the hundred weird forms Curran would have to face.

In his condition, that would be bad. He turned the other way, and led Curran back up to the drive room. Bedzyk waved at a control chair. "Have a seat."

Curran looked collegiate-boy shook up. He sank into the chair, again touching his chest in disbelief. "I've been like this for over two months ... they haven't found out yet; I've tried to keep myself from showing it ..."

He was shivering wildly.

Bedzyk perched on the shelf of the plot tank, and crossed his legs. He folded his arms across his huge chest and looked at Curran. "What do they want down there? What do they want from their beloved Discards?" He savored the last word with the taste of alum.

"It's, it's so bad you won't believe it, Bedzyk." He ran a hand through his crew cut, nervously. "We thought we had the Sickness licked. There was every reason to believe the atmosphere spray Terra Pharmaceuticals developed would end it. They sprayed the entire planet, but something they didn't even know was in the spray, and something they only half-suspected in the Sickness, combined and produced a healthier strain.

"That was when it started getting bad. What had been a hit-and-miss thing—with just a few like yourselves, with some weakness in your bloodstreams making you susceptible—became a rule instead of an exception. People started changing while you watched. I—I—" he faltered again, shuddered at a memory.

"My, my fiancée," he went on, looking at his attaché case and his hands, "I was eating lunch with her in Rockefeller Plaza's Skytop. We had to be back at work in Butte in twenty minutes, just time to catch a cab, and she—she—changed while we were sitting there. Her eyes, they, they—I can't explain it, you can't know what it was like seeing them water and run down her ch-cheeks like that, it was—" his face tightened up as though he were trying to keep himself from going completely insane.

Bedzyk sharply curbed the hysteria. "We have seven people like that on board right now. I know what you mean. And they aren't the worst. Go on, you were saying?"

Such prosaic acceptance of the horror brought Curran's frenzy down. "It got so bad everyone was staying in the sterile shelters. The streets always empty; it was horrible. Then some quack physician out in Cincinnati or somewhere like that came up with an answer. A serum made from a secretion in the bloodstreams of—of—"

Bedzyk added the last word for him: "Of Discards?"

Curran nodded soberly.

Bedzyk's hard-edged laugh rattled against Curran's thin film of calm. He jerked his eyes to the man sitting on the plot tank. A furious expression came over him.

"What are you laughing at? We need your help! We need all you people as blood donors."

Bedzyk stopped laughing abruptly. "Why not use the changed ones from down there?" He jerked a thumb at the big Lucite viewport where Earth hung swollen and multicolored. "What's wrong with them—" and he added with malice "—with you?" Curran twitched as he realized he could so easily be lumped in with the afflicted.

"We're no good. We were changed by this new mutated Sickness. The secretion is different in our blood than it is in yours. You were stricken by the primary Sickness, or virus, or whatever they call it. We have a complicated one. But the way the research has outlined it, the only ones who have what we need, are you Dis—" he caught himself "—you people who were shipped out before the Sickness itself mutated."

Bedzyk snorted contemptuously. He let a wry, astonished smirk tickle his lips. "You Earthies are fantastic." He shook his head in private amusement.

He slipped off the plot tank's ledge and turned to the port, talking half to himself, half to a nonexistent third person in the drive room. "These Earthies are unbelievable! Can you imagine, can you *picture* it?" Astonishment rang in his disbelief at the proposal. "First they hustle us into a metal prison and shoot us out here to die alone, they don't want any part of us, go away, they say. Then, when the trouble comes to them too big, they run after us, can you help us please, you dirty, ugly things, help us nice clean Earthies." He spun suddenly. "Get out of here! Get off this ship! We won't help you.

"You have your allotments and your quotas for each world—"

Curran broke in, "Yes, that's it. If the population goes down much more, they've been killing themselves, riots, it's terrible, then the balance will be changed, and our entire System culture will bend and fall and—"

Bedzyk cut him off, finishing what he had been saying, "—yes, you have your dirty little quotas, but you have no room for us. Well, we've got no room for you! Now get the hell off this ship. We don't want to help you!"

Curran leaped to his feet. "You can't send me away like this! You don't speak for all of them aboard. You can't treat a Terran emissary this way—" Bedzyk had him by the jumper, and had propelled him toward the closed companionway door before the attaché knew quite what was happening. He hit the door and rebounded. As he stumbled back toward Bedzyk, the great-chested mutant snatched the briefcase from beside the control chair and slammed it into Curran's stomach. "Here! Here's your offer and your lousy demands, and get off this ship! We don't want any part of y—"

The door crashed open, and the Discards were there.

They filled the corridor, as far back as the angle where cross-passages ran off toward the saloon and galley. They shoved and nudged each other to get a view into the drive room; Samswope and Harmony Teat and Dresden were in the front, and from somewhere Samswope had produced an effectively deadly little rasp-pistol. He held it tightly, threateningly, and Bedzyk felt flattered that they had come to his aid.

"You don't need that, Sam—Mr. Curran was just leav—"

Then he realized. The rasp was pointed not at Curran, but at him.

He stood frozen, one hand still clutching Curran's sleeve, as Curran bellied the briefcase to himself.

"Dresden overheard it all, Mr. Curran," Samswope said in a pathetically ingratiating tone. "*He* wants us to rot on this barge." He gestured at Bedzyk with his free hand as the dumb head nodded certain agreement. "What offer can you make us, can we go home, Mr. Curran ...?" There was a whimpering and a pleading in Samswope's voice that Bedzyk had only *sensed* before.

He tried to break in, "Are you insane, Swope? Putty, that's all you are! Putty when you see a fake hope that you'll get off this ship! Can't you see they just want to *use* us? Can't you understand that?"

Samswope's face grew livid and he screamed, "Shut up! Just shut up and let Curran talk! We don't want to die on this ship. *You* may like it, you little tin god, but we hate it here! So shut up and let him talk!"

Curran spoke rapidly then: "If you allow us to send a medical detachment up here to use you as blood donors, I have the word of the System Central that you will all be allowed to land on Earth and we'll have a reservation for you so you can live some kind of normal lives again—"

"Hey, what's the matter with you?" Bedzyk again burst in, trying vainly to speak over the hubbub from the corridor. "Can't you see he's lying? They'll use us and then desert us again!"

Samswope growled menacingly, "If you don't shut up I'll kill you, Bedzyk!"

Bedzyk faltered into silence and watched the scene before him. They were melting. They were going to let this rotten turncoat Earthie blind them with false hopes.

"We've worked our allotments around so there is space for you, perhaps in the new green-valleys of South America or on the veldtland in Rhodesia. It will be wonderful, but we need your blood, we need your help."

"Don't trust him! Don't believe him, you can't believe an Earthman!" Bedzyk shouted, stumbling forward to wrest the rasp-pistol from Samswope's grip.

Samswope fired point-blank. First the rasp of the power spurting from the muzzle of the tiny pistol filled the drive room, then the smell of burning flesh, and Bedzyk's eyes opened wide in pain. He screamed thinly, and staggered back against Curran. Curran stepped aside, and Bedzyk mewed in agony, and crumpled onto the deck. A huge hole had been seared through his huge chest. Huge chest, huge death, and he lay there with his eyes open, barely forming

104

the words "Don't ... you can't, can't t-trust an Earth-mmm ..." with his bloody lips. The last word formed and became a forever intaglio.

Curran's face had paled out till it was a blotch against the dark blue of his jumper. "Y-y-y ..."

Samswope moved into the drive room and took Curran by the sleeve, almost where Bedzyk had held it. "You promise us we can land and be allowed to settle someplace on Earth?"

Curran nodded dumbly. Had they asked for Earth in its socket, he would have nodded agreement. Samswope still held the rasp.

"All right, then ... get your med detachment up here, and get that blood. We want to go home, Mr. Curran, we want to go home more than anything!"

They led him to the lock. Behind him, Curran saw three mutants lifting the blasted body of Bedzyk, bearing it on their shoulders through the crowd. The body was borne out of sight down a cross-corridor, and Curran followed it out of sight with his eyes.

Beside him, Samswope said: "To the garbage lock. We go that way, Mr. Curran." His tones were hard and uncompromising. "We don't like going that way, Mr. Curran. We want to go home. You'll see to it, won't you, Mr. Curran?"

Curran again nodded dumbly, and entered the lock linking ships.

Ten hours later, the med detachment came up. The Discards were completely obedient and tremendously helpful.

It took nearly eleven months to inoculate the entire population of the Earth and the rest of the System—strictly as preventative caution dictated—and during that time no more Discards took their lives. Why should they? They were going home. Soon the tug ships would come, and help jockey the big Discard vessel into orbit for the run to Earth. They were going home. There was room for them now, even in their condition. Spirits ran high, and laughter tinkled oddly down the passageway in the "evenings." There was even a wedding between Arkay (who was blind and had a bushy tail) and a pretty young thing the others called Daanae, for she could not speak herself. Without a mouth that was impossible. At the ceremony in the saloon, Samswope acted as minister, for the Discards had made him their leader in the same silent way they had made Bedzyk the leader before him. Spirits ran high, and the constant knowledge that as soon as Earth had the Sickness under control they would be going home, kept them patient; eleven months.

Then one "afternoon" the ship came.

Not the little tugs, as they had supposed, but a cargo ship nearly as big as their own home. Samswope rushed to synch in the locks, and when the red lights merged on the board, he locked the two together firmly, and scrambled back through the throng to be the first to greet the men who would deliver them.

105

When the lock sighed open, and they saw the first ten who had been thrust in, they knew the truth.

One had a head flat as a plate, with no eyes, and its mouth in its neck. Another had several hundred thousand slimy tentacles where arms should have been, and waddled on stumps that could never again be legs. Still another was brought in by a pair of huge empty-faced men, in a bowl. The bowl contained a yellow jelly, and swimming in the yellow jelly was the woman.

Then they knew. They were not going home. As lockful after lockful of more Discards came through, to swell their ranks even more, they knew these were the last of the tainted ones from Earth. The last ones who had been stricken by the Sickness—who had changed before the serum could save them. These were the last, and now the Earth was clean.

Samswope watched them trail in, some dragging themselves on appendageless torsos, others in baskets, still others with one arm growing from a chest, or hair that was blue and fungus growing out all over the body. He watched them and knew the man he had killed had been correct. For among the crowd he glimpsed a bare-chested Discard with huge sores on his body. Curran.

And as the cargo ship unlocked and swept back to Earth—with the silent warning *Don't follow us, don't try to land, there's no room for you here*—Samswope could hear Bedzyk's hysterical tones in his head:

Don't trust them! There is room for us anywhere! Don't trust them!

You can't trust an Earthman!

Samswope started walking slowly toward the galley, knowing he would need someone to seal the garbage lock after him. But it didn't matter who it was. There were more than enough Discards aboard now.

Pain. The pain of being obsolete. I go down to Santa Monica sometimes, and walk along through the oceanside park that forms the outermost edge of California. There, at the shore of the Pacific, like flotsam washed up by America, with no place to go, are the old people. Their time has gone, their eyes look out across the water for another beginning, but they have come to the final moments. They sit in the vanilla sunshine and they dream of yesterday. Kind old people, for the most part. They talk to each other, they talk to themselves, and they wonder where it all went.

I stop and sit on the benches and talk to them sometimes. Not often, it makes me think of endings rather than continuations or new beginnings. They're sad, but they have a nobility that cannot be ignored. They're passed-over, obsolescent, but they still run well and they have good minutes in them. Their pain is a terrible thing because it cries to be given the chance to work those arthritic fingers at something meaningful, to work those brain cells at something challenging.

This story is about someone in the process of being passed-over, being made obsolete. He fights. I would fight. Some of the old people in Santa Monica fight. Do we ever win? Against the shadow that inevitably falls, no.

Against the time between now and the shadow's arrival, yes, certainly.

That's the message in

107

Wanted in Surgery

CHAPTER ONE

A man named Tibor Károly Zsebok, who had escaped from the People's Hungarian Protectorate to the North American Continent's sanctuary late in the year 2087, invented it. While working as a bonded technician for the Orrin Tool and Tree Conglomerate—on a design to create a robot capable of fine watch repairs—he discovered the factor of multiple choice. He was able to apply this concept to the cellulose-plasteel brain of his watch repair robot's pilot model, and came up with the startling "physician mechanical." Infinitely more intricate than a mere robot-mechanical, yet far simpler than a human brain, it was capable—after proper conditioning—of the most delicate of operations. Further, the "phymech," as it was tagged soon after, was capable of infallible diagnosis, involving anything organic.

The mind was still locked to the powers of the metal physician, but for the ills of the body there was no more capable administrator.

Zsebok died several weeks after his pilot model had been demonstrated at a special closed session of the House of Congress; from a coronary thrombosis.

But his death was more of a propelling factor to widespread recognition of the phymech than his life could ever have been.

The House of Congress appointed a committee of fact-finders, from the firm of Data, Unlimited—who had successfully completed the Orinoco Basin Probe—and compared their three-month findings with the current Histophysiology appropriations allocated to the Secretary of Medicine.

They found phymechs could be operated in all the socialized hospitals of the Continent, for far less than was being spent on doctors' salaries.

After all, a doctor continued to *need.*

A phymech absorbed one half pint of liquified radiol every three years, and an occasional lubrication, to insure proper functioning.

So the government passed a law. The Hippocratic Law of 2088, which said in essence:

"All ministrations shall henceforth be confined to government-sponsored hospitals; emergency cases necessitating attendance outside said institutions shall be handled *only*, repeat *only*, by registered Physician Mechanicals issuing from registered hospital pools. Any irregularities or deviations from this procedure shall be handled as cases outside the law, and illegal attendance by non-Mechanical Physicians shall be severely punishable by cancellation of practicing license and/or fine and imprisonment ..."

Johns Hopkins was the first to be defranchised. Then the Columbia School of Medicine, and the other colleges followed shortly thereafter.

A few specialist schools were maintained for a time; but it became increasingly apparent after the first three years of phymech operation that even the specialists were slow compared to the robot doctors. So even they passed away. Doctors who had been licensed before the innovations the phymechs brought, were maintained at slashed salaries and were reduced to assistants, interns.

They were, however, given a few annuities, which boiled down eventually to 1) a franking privilege so postage was unnecessary on their letters; 2) a small annual dole; 3) subscriptions to current medical journals (now filled more with electronic data pertinent to phymechs than surgical techniques); and 4) honorary titles. Doctors in title only.

There was dissatisfaction.

In 2091 Kohlbenschlagg, the greatest brain surgeon of them all, died. He passed away on a quiet October morning, with the climate dome purring ever so faintly above the city, and the distant scream of the transport sphincter opening to allow the Earth-Mars 8:00 liner through. A quiet, drawn-faced man with a great talent in slim fingers. He died in his sleep, and the papers clacked out of the homeslots, with heavy black headlines across yellow plastic sheets. But not about Kohlbenschlagg. He was yesterday's news. The headline was about the total automation changeover in the Ford-Chrysler plants.

On page one hundred and eighteen there was a five-line obituary that labeled him "a prephymech surgeon of some skill." It also reported he had died of acute alcoholism.

It was not specifically true.

His death was caused by a composite. Acute alcoholism.

And a broken heart.

He died alone, but he was remembered. By the men and women who, like Kohlbenschlagg, had spent their early lives in dedication to the staff and the lion's head, the hand and eagle's eye. By men and women who could not adjust. The small legion of men and women who still walked the antiseptic corridors of the hospitals.

Men like Stuart Bergman, M.D.

This is his story.

CHAPTER TWO

The main operation theater of Memorial was constructed along standard lines. The observation bubble was set high on one wall, curving large and down, with a separating section allowing two viewing stands. The operating stage, on a telescoping base that raised or lowered it for easier observation from the bubble, squatted in the center of the room. There were no operating lamps in the ceiling, as in old-style hospitals, for the phymechs had their powerful eternalight mounted atop their heads, serving their needs more accurately than any outside light source could have.

Beyond the stage, there were anaesthetic spheres clipped to the walls—in five-container groups—where they could be easily reached should the phymech's personal supply run dry, and a rapidroll belt running from a digital supply machine beside the operating table to the see-through selector cabinets that stood by the exits.

That was all; everything that was needed.

Even the spheres and extra cabinets might have been dispensed with; but somehow they had been maintained, just slightly limiting the phymech's abilities. As though to reassure some unnamed person that they needed help. Even if it was mechanical help to help the mechanicals.

The three phymechs were performing the operation directly beneath the bubble when Bergman came in. The bubble was dark, but he could see Murray Thomas's craggy features set against the light of the operating stage. The illumination had been a concession to the human observers, for with their own eternalights, the phymechs could work in a total blackout during a power failure.

Bergman held the crumpled news sheet in his hand, page one hundred and eighteen showing, and stared at the scene below him.

Naturally, it *would* be a brain operation today! The one day it should be a mere goiter job, or a plantar stripping, if just to keep him steady; but no, it *had* to be a brain job, with the phymech's thirty telescoping, snakelike appendages extruded and snicking into the patient.

Bergman swallowed hard, and made his way down the slope of aisle to the empty seat beside Thomas. He was a dark man, with an almost unnaturally spadelike face. High, prominent cheekbones, giving him a gaunt look, and veins that stood out along the temples. His nose was thin and humped where it had been broken years before.

His eyes were deep and darkest blue, so they appeared black. His hair was thin, roughly combed; back from the forehead without affectation or wave, just combed, because he had to keep the hair from his eyes.

He slumped into the seat, keeping his eyes off the operation below, keeping the face of Murray Thomas in his sight, with the light from below playing up across the round, unflustered features. He held out the news sheet, touching Thomas's arm with it; for the first time, as the young doctor started, Thomas realized Bergman was there. He turned slowly, and his placid stare met the wild look of Bergman; a question began to form, but Thomas cast a glance behind him, toward the top of the seat tier, at the silent dark bulk of the head resident. He put a hand on Bergman's arm, and then he saw the news sheet.

Bergman offered it another inch, and Thomas took it. He opened it out, turning it below the level of the seats, trying to catch the light from below. He roamed the page for a moment, then his hands crumpled tight on the plastic. He saw the five-line filler.

Kohlbenschlagg was dead.

He turned to Bergman, and his eyes held infinite sorrow. He mouthed with his lips the words, "I'm sorry, Stuart," but they died midway between them.

He stared at Bergman's face for a moment, knowing he could do nothing for the man now. Kohlbenschlagg had been Stuart Bergman's teacher, his friend, more a father to him than the father Bergman had run away from in his youth. Now Bergman was totally alone ... for his wife, Thelma, was no help in this situation ... her constitution could not cope with a case of inner disintegration.

With difficulty he turned back to the operation, feeling an overwhelming desire to take Bergman's hand, to help ease away the sorrow he knew coursed through the man; but the sorrow was a personal thing, and he was cut off from the tense man beside him.

111

Bergman watched the operation now. There was nothing else to do. He had spent ten years of his life training to be a physician, and now he was sitting watching faceless blocks of metal do those ten years better than he ever could.

Murray Thomas was abruptly aware of heavy breathing beside him. He did not turn his head. He had seen Bergman getting nearer and nearer the cracking point for weeks now: ever since the phymechs had been completely installed, and the human doctors had been relegated to assistants, interns, instrument-carriers. He feverishly hoped this was not the moment Bergman would choose to fall apart.

The phymechs below were proceeding with the delicate operation. One of the telescoping, snakelike tentacles of one phymech had a wafer-thin circular saw on it, and as Thomas watched, the saw sliced down, and they could hear the buzz of steel meeting skull.

"God in *heaven!* Stop it, stop it, stop it ...!"

Thomas was an instant too late. Bergman was up out of his seat, down the aisle, and banging his fists against the clear plasteel of the observation bubble, before he could be stopped.

It produced a feeling of utter hysteria in the bubble, as though all of them wanted to scream, had been holding it back, and now were struggling with the sounds, not to join in. Bergman battered himself up against the clearness of the bubble, mumbling, screaming, his face a riot of pain and horror.

"Not even a ... a ... decent *death!*" he was screaming. "He lies down there, and rotten dirty metal *things* ... things, God dammit! *Things* rip up his patients! Oh, God, where is the way, where, where, where ... "

Then the three interns erupted from the door at the top rear of the bubble, and ran down the aisle. In an instant they had Bergman by the shoulders, the arms, the neck, and were dragging him back up the aisle.

Calkins, the head resident, yelled after them, "Take him to my office for observation, I'll be right there."

Murray Thomas watched his friend disappear in the darkness toward the rectangle of light in the rear wall. Then he was gone, and Thomas heard Calkins say: "Ignore that outburst, doctors, there is always someone who gets squeamish at the sight of a well-performed operation."

Then he was gone, off to examine Bergman.

And Murray Thomas felt a brassy, bitter taste on his tongue; Bergman afraid of blood, the sight of an operation? Not likely. He had seen Stuart Bergman work many times—not Stuart Bergman; the operating room was home to Bergman. No, it hadn't been that.

Then it was that Thomas realized: the incident had completely shattered the mood and attention of the men in the bubble. *They* were incapable of watering the phymechs any further today—but the phymechs ...

... they were undisturbed, unseeing, uncaring: calmly, coolly working, taking off the top of the patient's skull.

Thomas felt desperately ill.

CHAPTER THREE

"Honest to God, I tell you, Murray, I can't take it much longer!"

Bergman was still shaking from the examination in Calkins's offices. His hands were prominent with blue veins, and they trembled ever so slightly across the formatop of the table. The dim sounds of the Medical Center filtered to them in the bush—booth. Bergman ran a hand through his hair. "Every time I see one of those ..." he paused, hesitated, then did not use the word. Murray Thomas knew the word, had it come forth, would have been *monsters*. Bergman went on, a blank space in his sentence, "Every time I see one of them picking around inside one of my patients, with those metal tips, I—I get sick to my stomach! It's all I can do to keep from ripping out its god-damned wiring!" His face was deathly pale, yet somehow unnaturally flushed.

He quivered as he spoke. And quivered again.

Dr. Murray Thomas put out a hand placatingly. "Now take it easy, Stu. You keep getting yourself all hot over this thing and if it doesn't break you—which it damned well easily could—they'll revoke your license, bar you from practicing." He looked across at Bergman, and blinked assuringly, as if to keynote his warning.

Bergman muttered with surliness, "Fine lot of practicing I do now. Or you, for that matter."

Thomas tapped a finger on the table. It caused the multicolored bits of plastic beneath the formatop, to jiggle, casting pinpoints of light across Bergman's strained features. "And besides, Stu, you have no *logical*, scientific reason for hating the phymechs."

Bergman stared back angrily. "Science doesn't come into it, and you know it. This is from the gut, Murray, not the brain!"

"Look, Stu, they're infallible; they're safer and they can do a job quicker with less mess than even a—a Kohlbenschlagg. Right?"

Bergman nodded reluctantly, but there was a dangerous edge to his expression. "But at least Kohlbenschlagg, even with those thick-lensed glasses, was *human*. It wasn't like having a piece of—of—well, a piece of *stovepipe* rummaging around in a patient's stomach."

He shook his head sadly in remembrance. "Old Fritz couldn't take it. That's what killed him. Those damned machines. Playing intern to a phymech was too much for him—Oh *hell!* You know what a grand heart that old man had, Murray. Fifty years in medicine and then to be barely *allowed* to hold sponge for a lousy tick-tock ... and what was worse, knowing the tick-tock could hold the sponge more firmly with one of its pincers. That's what killed old Fritz."

Bergman added softly, staring at his shaking hands, "And at that ... *he's* the lucky one."

And then. "We're the damned of our culture, Murray; the kept men of medicine."

Thomas looked up startled, then annoyed. "Oh, for Christ's sake, Stuart, stop being melodramatic. Nothing of the sort. If a better scalpel comes along, do you refuse to discard the old issue because you've used it so long? Don't be an ass."

"*But we're not scalpels. We're men! We're doctors!*" He was on his feet suddenly, as though the conversation had been physically building in him, forcing an explosion. The two whiskey glasses slipped and dumped as his thighs banged the table in rising. Bergman's voice was raised, and his temples throbbed, yet he was not screaming; even so, the words came out louder than any scream.

"For God's sake, Stu, *sit down!*" Thomas looked apprehensively around the Medical Center Lounge. "If the head resident should walk in, we'd *both* get our throats cut. Sit *down*, will you already!"

Bergman slumped slowly back onto the form seat. It depressed and flowed around him caressingly, and he squirmed in agony, as though it were strangling him. Even after he was fully seated, his shoulders continued rounding; his eyes were wild. Beads of perspiration stood out on his forehead, his upper lip.

Thomas leaned forward, a frown creasing his mouth. "Take hold, Stu. Don't let a thing like this ruin you. Better men than us have felt this way about it, but you can't stop progress. And losing your head, doing something crazy like that exhibition at the operation yesterday, won't do any of us any good. It's all we can do to maintain what rights we have left. It's a bad break for us, Stu, but it's good for the whole rest of the human race, and dammit, man, they come before us. It's as simple as that."

He drew a handkerchief from his breast pouch and mopped at the spreading twin pools of liquor, covertly watching Bergman from behind lowered lashes.

The sudden blare of a juke brought Bergman's head up, his nostrils flaring. When he realized what it was, he subsided, the lights vanishing from his eyes.

He rested his head in his hand, rubbing slowly up and down the length of his nose. "How did it all start, Murray? I mean, all this?" He looked at the roaring juke that nearly drowned out conversation despite the hush booth ... the bar with its mechanical drink interpolater—remarkable mnemonic

114

circuits capable of mixing ten thousand different liquors flawlessly—and intoxication estimater ... the fully mechanized hospital rearing huge outside the plasteel-fronted bar ... robot physicians glimpsed occasionally passing before a lighted window.

Windows showing light only because the human patients and fallible doctors needed it. The robots needed no light; they needed no fame, and no desire to help mankind. All they needed was their power pack and an occasional oiling. In return for which they saved mankind.

Bergman's mind tossed the bitter irony about like a dog with a foul rag in its mouth.

Murray Thomas sighed softly, considered Bergman's question. He shook his head. "I don't know, Stu." The words paced themselves, emerging slowly, reluctantly. "Perhaps it was the automatic pilot, or the tactical computers they used in the Third War, or maybe even farther back than that; maybe it was as far back as electric sewing machines, and hydramatic shift cars and self-serve elevators. It was machines, and they worked better than humans. That was it, pure and simple. A hunk of metal is nine times out of ten better than a fallible man."

Thomas considered what he had said, added definitely, "I'll take that back: *ten* times out of ten. There's nothing a cybernetics man can't build into one of those things now. It was inevitable they'd get around to taking human lives out of the hands of mere men." He looked embarrassed for an instant at the length and tone of his reply, then sighed again and downed the last traces of his drink, running his tongue absently around the lip of the glass, tasting the dried liquid there.

Bergman's intensity seemed to pulse, grow stronger. He was obviously trying to find an answer to the problem of himself, within himself. He hunched further over, looking into his friend's face earnestly, almost boyishly, "But— but it doesn't seem *right*, somehow. We've always depended on doctors— human doctors—to care for the sick and dying. It was a constant, Murray. A something you could depend on. In time of war a doctor was inviolate.

"In times of need—I know it sounds maudlin, Murray—for God's sake, in times of need a doctor was priest and father and teacher and patriot, and ... and ..."

He made futile motions with his hands, as though pleading the words to appear from the air. Then he continued in a stronger voice, from a memory ground into his mind:

"'I will keep pure and holy both my life and my art. In whatsoever houses I enter, I will enter to help the sick, and I will abstain from all intentional wrongdoing and harm. And whatsoever I shall see or hear in the course of my profession in my intercourse with men, if it be what should not be published abroad, I will never divulge, holding such things to be holy secrets.'"

Thomas's eyebrows rose slightly as his lips quirked in an unconscious smile. He had known Bergman would resort to the Oath eventually. Dedicated wasn't enough of a word to describe Stuart Bergman, it seemed. He was right, it *was* maudlin, and still ...

Bergman continued. "What good is it all now? They've only had the phymechs a few years now, only a few, and they have them in solidly ... even though there are things about them they aren't sure about. So what good were all the years in school, in study, in tradition? We can't even go into the homes any more."

His face seemed to grow more haggard under the indirect gleam of the glaze lights in the lounge; his hair seemed grayer than a moment before; the lines of his face were deeper. He swallowed nervously, ran a finger through the faint coating of wet left by the spilled drinks. "What kind of a practice is that? To carry slop buckets? To be allowed to watch as the robots cut and sew our patients? To be kept behind glass at the big operations?

"To see the red lights flash on the hot board and know a mobilized monster is rolling faster than an ambulance to the scene? Is that what you're telling me I have to adjust to? Are you, Murray? Don't expect me to be as calm about it as you!"

"And most degrading of all," he added, as if to solidify his arguments, "to have them throw us a miserable appendectomy or stomach-pump job once a week. Like scraps from the table ... and watch us while we do it! What *are* we, dogs? To be treated like pets? I tell you, I'm going crazy, Murray! I go home at night and find myself even cutting my steak as though it were heart tissue. Anything, anything at all, just to remind myself that I was trained for surgery. My God! When I think of all the years, all the sweat, all the gutting and starving, just to come to this! Murray, where's it going to end?"

He was on the verge of another scene like the one in the operating room observation bubble.

Whatever had happened when the Head Resident had examined Bergman—and it *seemed* to have been cleared up, for Bergman was still scheduled on the boards as phymech assistant, though his weekly operation had been set ahead three days—it wouldn't do to let it flare up again.

And Murray Thomas knew things were boiling inside his ex-schoolmate; he had no idea how long it would be before the lid blew off, ruining Bergman permanently.

"Calm down, Stuart," he said. "Let me dial you another drink ..."

"Don't touch that goddam mechanical thing!" he roared, striking Thomas's hand from the interpolater dial.

He gasped raggedly. "There are *some* things a machine *can't* do. Machines brush my teeth in the morning, and they cook my food, and they lull me to

116

sleep, but there must be *something* they can't do better than a human ... otherwise why did God create humans? To be waited on by tin cans? I don't know what they are, but I swear there must be some abilities a human possesses that a robot doesn't. There must be something that makes a man more valuable than a whirring, clanking chunk of tin!" He stopped, out of breath. It was then that Calkins, the head resident, stepped around the panel separating the booths from the bar.

The head resident stood there silently, watching for a moment, like a hound on point. He fingered the lapel on his sport jumper absently. "Getting a bit noisy, aren't you, Dr. Bergman?"

Stuart Bergman's face was alive with fear. His eyes lowered to his hands; entwined like serpents, seeking sanctuary in each other, white with the pressure of his clasping, his fingers writhed. "I—I was just, just, airing a few views ... that's all, Dr. Calkins."

"Rather nasty views, I must say, Dr. Bergman. Might be construed as dissatisfaction with the way I'm handling things at Memorial. You wouldn't want anyone to think that, would you, Dr. Bergman?" His words had taken on the tone of command, of steel imbedded in rock.

Bergman shook his head quickly, slightly, nervously. "No. No, I didn't mean that at all, Dr. Calkins. I was just—well, you know. I thought perhaps if we physicians had a few more operations, a few more difficult ..."

"Don't you think the phymechs are quite capable of handling any such, Dr. Bergman?"

There was an air of expectancy in his voice ... waiting for Bergman to say the wrong thing. *That's* what you'd like, wouldn't you, Calkins? *That's* what you want! His thoughts spun sidewise, madly.

"I suppose so ... yes, I know they are. It was, well, it's difficult to remember I'm a doctor, not doing any work for so long and all, and ..."

"That's about enough, Bergman!" snapped Calkins. "The government subsidized the phymechs, and they use taxpayers' money to keep them serviced and saving lives. They have a finer record than *any* human ..."

Bergman broke in sharply. "But they haven't been fully tested or ..."

Calkins stared him into silence, replied, "If you want to remain on the payroll, remain in the hospital, Dr. Bergman, even as an assistant, you'd better tone down and watch yourself, Bergman. We have our eyes on you."

"But I ..."

"I said that's enough, Bergman!" Turning to Murray Thomas he added violently, "And I'd watch who I keep company with, Thomas, if I were you. That's all. Good evening." He strode off lightly, almost jauntily, arrogance in each step, leaving Bergman huddled in a corner of the booth, staring wild-eyed at his hands.

117

"Rotten lousy appointee!" snarled Thomas softly. "If it weren't for his connections with the secretary of medicine, he'd be in the same boat with us. The lousy bastard."

"I—I guess I'd better be getting home," mumbled Bergman, sliding out of the booth. A sudden blast from the juke shivered him, and he regained his focus on Thomas with difficulty. "Thelma's probably waiting dinner for me.

"Thanks ... thanks for having a drink with me, Murray. I'll see you at washup tomorrow." He ran a finger down the front of his jumper, sealing the suit; he pulled up his collar, sealing the suit to the neck.

A fine spray of rain—scheduled for this time by Weatherex—was dotting the huge transparent front of the lounge, and Bergman stared at it, engrossed for an instant, as though seeing something deeper in the rain.

He drew a handful of octagonal plastic chits from his pouch, dropped them into the pay slot on his side of the table, and started away. The machine registered an overpayment, but he did not bother to collect the surplus coins.

He paused, turned for a moment. Then, "Thanks ... Murray ..." and he was gone into the rain.

Poor slob, thought Dr. Murray Thomas, an ache beginning to build within him for things he could not name. *Just can't adjust*. He knew he couldn't hold it, but he dialed another drink. He regretted it while doing it, but that ache had to be avoided at all costs. The drink was a double.

CHAPTER FOUR

That night was hell. Hell with the torture of memories past and present. He knew he had been acting like a fool, that he was just another stupid man who could not accept what was to be.

But there was more, and it pervaded his thoughts, his dreams. He had been a coward in front of Calkins. He felt strongly—God! More than merely strongly!—yet he had backed down. After making an ass of himself at the operation, the day of old Fritz Kohlbenschlagg's death, he had backed down. He had run away from his problem.

Now, all the years that he had lived by the Oath were wasted. His life seemed to be a failure. He had struggled desperately to get where he was, and now that he was there ... he was nowhere. He had run away.

It was the first time since he had been very young that he had felt that way. He lay on the bed, the formkling sheet rumpled half on the floor at the foot of the bed. Thelma lay silent in the other hush-bunk, the blanker keeping her snores from disturbing him. And the memories slid by slowly.

118

He could still remember the time a friend had fallen into a cistern near a deserted house—before the dome—and fear had prevented his descending to save his playmate. The boy had drowned, and ten-year-old Stuart Bergman had fostered a guilt of that failure he had carried ever since. It had, he sometimes thought, been one of the factors that had contributed to his decision to become a doctor.

Now again, years later, he was helpless and trembling in the spider's mesh of a situation in which he could not move to do what he knew was right. He did not know why he was so set against them—Murray's analogy of the scalpel was perfectly valid—but something sensed but unnamed in his guts told him he was right. This was unnatural, damnable, that humans were worked over by machines.

It somehow—irrationally—seemed a plan of the Devil. He had heard people call the machines the Devil's Playthings. Perhaps they were right. He lay on his bed, sweating.

Feeling incomplete, feeling filthy, feeling contaminated by his own inadequacy, and his cowardice before Calkins.

He screwed his face up in agony, in self-castigation, shutting his eyes tight, till the nerves running through his temples throbbed.

Then he placed the blame where it really belonged.

Why was he suffering? Why was his once-full life so suddenly empty and framed by worthlessness? Fear. Fear of what? Why was he afraid? Because the phymechs had taken over.

Again. The same answer. And in his mind, his purpose resolved, solidified.

He had to get the phymechs discredited; had to find some reason for them to be thrown out. But how? How?

They *were* better. In all ways. Weren't they?

Three days later, as he assisted a phymech on his scheduled operating assignment, the answer came to Bergman as horribly as he might have wished. It came in the form of a practical demonstration, and he was never to forget it.

The patient had been involved in a thresher accident on one of the group-farms. The sucker-mouth thresher had whipped him off his feet, and dragged him in, feet first. He had saved himself from being completely chewed to bits by placing his hands around the mouth of the thresher, and others had rushed in to drag him free before his grip loosened.

He had fainted from pain, and luckily, for the sucker-mouth had ground off both his legs just below the knees. When they wheeled him before Bergman—with his oxygen-mask and tube in hand—and the phymech—with instruments already clasped in nine of its thirteen magnetic tips—the man was covered with a sheet.

119

Bergman's transparent face-mask quivered as he drew back the sheet, exposing the man. They had bound up the stumps, and cauter-halted the bleeding ... but the patient was as badly off as Bergman had ever seen an injured man.

It will be close all the way. Thank God, in this case, the phymech is fast and efficient. No human could save this one in time.

So intent was he on watching the phymech's technique, so engrossed was he at the snicker and gleam of the instruments being whipped from their cubicles in the phymech's storage-bin chest, he failed to adjust the anaesthesia-cone properly. Bergman watched the intricate play of the phymech's tentacles, as they telescoped out and back from the small holes in each shoulder-globe. He watched the tortured flesh being stripped back to allow free play for the sutures. The faint hiss of the imperfectly fitted cone reached him too late.

The patient sat up, suddenly.

Straight up, with hands rigid to the table. His eyes opened, and he stared down at the ripped and bloodied stumps where his legs had been.

His screams echoed back from the operating room walls.

"Oh, I wanna die, I wanna die, I wanna die ..." Over and over his hysterical screams beat at Bergman's consciousness. The phymech automatically moved to leach off the rising panic in the patient, but it was too late. The patient fainted, and almost instantly the cardio showed a dip. The spark was going out.

The phymech ignored it; there was nothing it could do about it. Organically the man was being handled efficiently. The trouble was emotional ... where the phymech never went.

Bergman stared in horror. The man was dying ... right out from under the tentacles. *Why doesn't the thing try to help the man? Why doesn't he soothe him, let him know it'll be all right? He's dying, because he's in shock ... he doesn't want to live! Just a word would do ...*

Bergman's thoughts whipped themselves into a frenzy, but the phymech continued operating, calmly, hurriedly, but with the patient failing rapidly.

Bergman started forward, intent to reach the patent. The injured man had looked up and seen himself amputated bloodily just beneath the knees, and worse, had seen the faceless metal entity working over him; at that crucial moment when any little thing could sway the desire to live, the man had seen no human with whom he could identify ... merely a rounded and planed block of metal. He wanted to die.

Bergman reached out to touch the patient. Without ceasing its activities, the phymech extruded a chamois-mitt tentacle, and removed Bergman's hand. The hollow inflectionless voice of the robot darted from its throat-speaker:

"No interference please. This is against the rules."

Bergman drew back, horror stamped across his fine features, his skin literally crawling, from the touch of the robot, and from the sight of the phymech operating steadily ... on a corpse.

The man had lost the spark.

The operation was a success, as they had often quipped, but the patient was dead. Bergman felt nausea grip him with sodden fingers, and he doubled over turning quickly toward the wall. He stared up at the empty observation bubble, thankful this was a standard, routine operation and no viewers sat behind the clearness up there. He leaned against the feeder-trough of the instrument cabinets, and vomited across the sparkling grey plasteel tiles. A servomeck skittered free of its cubicle and cleaned away the mess immediately.

It only heightened his sickness.

Machines cleaning up for machines.

He didn't bother finishing as assistant on the phymech's grisly operation. It would do no good; and besides, the phymech didn't need any help.

It wasn't human.

Bergman didn't show up at Memorial for a week; there was a polite inquiry from Scheduling, but when Thelma told them he was "just under the weather," they replied "well, the robot doesn't really need him anyhow," and that was that. Stuart Bergman's wife was worried, however.

Her husband lay curled on the bed, face to the wall, and murmured the merest murmurs to her questions. It was really as though he had something on his mind.

(Well, if he *did*, why didn't he *say* something! There just is no understanding that man. Oh well, no time to worry over that now ... Francine and Sally are getting up the electro-mah jongg game at Sally's today. Dear, can you punch up some lunch for yourself? Well, really! Not even an answer, just that mumble. Oh well, I'd better hurry ...)

Bergman *did* have something on his mind. He had seen a terrifying and a gut-wrenching thing. He had seen the robot fail. Miserably fail. That was the sum of it. For the first time since he had been unconsciously introduced to the concept of phymech infallibility, he had seen it as a lie. The phymech was *not* perfect. The man had died under Bergman's eyes. Now Stuart Bergman had to reason why ... and whether it had happened before ... whether it would happen again ... what it meant ... and what it meant to him, as well as the profession, as well as the world.

The phymech had *known* the man was in panic; the robot had instantly lowered the adrenaline count ... but it had been more than that. Bergman had handled cases like that in the past, where improperly-delivered anaesthesia had allowed a patient to become conscious and see himself split open. But in

121

such cases he had said a few reassuring words, had run a hand over the man's forehead, his eyes, and strangely enough, that bit of bedside manner had been delivered in just such a proper way that the patient sank back peacefully into sleep.

But the robot had done nothing.

It had ministered to the body, while the mind shattered. Bergman had known, even as the man had seen his bloody stumps, that the operation would fail.

Why had it happened? Was this the first time a man had died under the tentacles of a phymech, and if the answer was no ... why hadn't he heard of it? When he stopped to consider, lost still in that horror maelstrom of memory and pain, he realized it was because the phymechs were still "undergoing observation." But while that went on—so sure were the manufacturers, and the officials of the Department of Medicine, that the phymechs were perfect—lives were being lost in the one way they could not be charged to the robots.

An intangible factor was involved.

It had been such a simple thing. Just to tell the man, "You'll be all right, fellow, take it easy. We'll have you out of here good as new in a little while ... just settle back and get some sleep ... and let me get my job done; we've got to work together, you know ..."

That was all, just that much, and the life that had been in that mangled body would not have been lost. But the robot had stood there ticking, efficiently repairing tissue.

While the patient died in hopelessness and terror.

Then Bergman realized what it was a human had, a robot did not. He realized what it was a human could do that a robot could not. And it was so simple, so damnably simple, he wanted to cry. It was the human factor. They could never make a robot physician that was perfect, because a robot could not understand the psychology of the human mind.

Bergman put it into simple terms ...

The phymechs just didn't have a bedside manner!

CHAPTER FIVE

Paths to destruction.

So many paths. So many answers. So many solutions, and which of them was the right one? Were any of them the right ones? Bergman had known he must find out, had known he must solve this problem by his own hand, for perhaps no one else's hand would turn to the problem ... until it was too late.

Each day that passed meant another life had passed.

And the thought cursed Bergman more than any personal danger. He had to try something; in his desperation, he came up with a plan of desperation.

He would kill one of his patients ...

Once every two weeks, a human was assigned his own operation. True, he was more supervised than assisted by the phymech on duty, and the case was usually only an appendectomy or simple tonsillectomy ... but it *was* an operation. And, Lord knew, the surgeons were grateful for any bone thrown them.

This was Bergman's day.

He had been dreading it for a week, thinking about it for a week, knowing what he must do for a week. But it had to be done. He didn't know what would happen to him, but it didn't really matter what was going on in their hospitals ...

But if anything was to be done, it would have to be done boldly, swiftly, sensationally. And now. Something as awful as this couldn't wait much longer: the papers had been running articles about the secretary of medicine's new Phymech Proposal. That would have been the end. It would have to be now. Right now, while the issue was important.

He walked into the operating room.

A standard simple operation. No one in the bubble.

The phymech assistant stood silently waiting by the feeder trough. As Bergman walked across the empty room, the cubicle split open across the way, and a rolling phymech with a tabletop—on which was the patient—hurried to the operating table. The machine lowered the tabletop to the operating slab, and bolted it down quickly. Then it rolled away.

Bergman stared at the patient, and for a minute his resolve left him. She was a thin young girl with laugh-lines in her face that could never be erased ... except by death.

Up till a moment ago Bergman had known he would do it, but now ... Now he had to see whom he was going to do this thing to, and it made his stomach feel diseased in him, his breath filled with the decay of foul death. He couldn't do it.

The girl looked up at him, and smiled with light blue eyes, and somehow Bergman's thoughts centered on his wife, Thelma, who was nothing like this sweet, frail child. Thelma, whose insensitivity had begun in his life as humorous, and decayed through the barren years of their marriage till it was now a millstone he wore silently. Bergman knew he couldn't do what had to be done. Not to this girl.

The phymech applied the anaesthesia cone from behind the girl's head. She caught one quick flash of tentacled metal, her eyes widened with blueness, and then she was asleep. When she awoke, her appendix would be removed.

Bergman felt a wrenching inside him. This was the time. With Calkins so suspicious of him, with the phymechs getting stronger every day, this might be the last chance.

He prayed to God silently for a moment, then began the operation. Bergman carefully made a longitudinal incision in the right lower quadrant of the girl's abdomen, about four inches long. As he spread the wound, he saw this would be just an ordinary job. No peritonitis ... they had gotten the girl in quickly, and it hadn't ruptured. This would be a simple job, eight or nine minutes at the longest.

Carefully, Bergman delivered the appendix into the wound. Then he securely tied it at the base, and feeling the tension of what was to come building in him, cut it across and removed it.

He began to close the abdominal walls tightly.

Then he asked God for forgiveness, and did what had to be done. It was not going to be such a simple operation, after all.

The scalpel was an electro-blade—thin as a whisper—and as he brought it toward the flesh, his plan ran through his mind. The spin of a bullet, the passage of a silver fish through quicksilver, the flick of a thought, but it was all there, in totality, completeness and madness ...

He would sever an artery, the robot would sense what was being done, and would shoulder in to repair the damage. Bergman would slash another vein, and the robot would work at two jobs. He would slash again, and again, and yet again, till finally the robot would overload, and freeze. Then Bergman would overturn the table, the girl would be dead, there would be an inquiry and a trial, and he would be able to blame the robot for the death ... and tell his story ... make them check it ... make them stop using phymechs till the problem had been solved.

All that as the electro-blade moved in his hand.

Then the eyes of the girl fastened to his own, closed for a moment to consider what he was doing. In the darkness of his mind, he saw those eyes and knew finally:

What good was it to win his point, if he lost his soul?

The electro-blade clattered to the floor.

He stood there unmoving, as the phymech rolled near silently beside him, and completed the routine closure.

He turned away, and left the operating room quickly.

He left the hospital shortly after, feeling failure huge in his throat. He had had his opportunity, and had not been brave enough to take it. But was that it? Was it another edge of that inner cowardice he had shown before? Or was it that he realized *nothing* could be worth the taking of an innocent girl's life? Ethics, softheartedness, what? His mind was a turmoil.

The night closed down stark and murmuring around Bergman. He stepped from the light blotch of the lobby, and the rain misted down over him, shutting him away from life and man and everything but the dark wool of his inner thoughts. It had been raining like this the night Calkins had intimidated him. Was it always to rain on him, throughout his days?

Only the occasional whirr of a heater ploughing invisibly across the sky overhead broke the steady machine murmur of the city. He crossed the silent street quickly.

The square block of darkness that was Memorial was dotted with the faint rectangles of windows. Lighted windows. The hollow laughter of bitterness bubbled up from his belly as he saw the lights. Concessions to Man ... always concessions by the Almighty God of the Machine.

Inside Bergman's mind, something was fighting to be free. He was finished now, he knew that. He had had the chance, but it had been the wrong chance. It could never be right if it started from something like that girl's death. He knew that, too ... finally. But what was there to do?

And the answer came back hollowly: *Nothing.*

Behind him, where he could not see it, a movement of metal in the shadows.

Bergman walked in shadows, also. Thoughts that were shadows. Thoughts that led him only to bleak futility and despair. The Zsebok Mechanical Physicians. *Phymechs.*

The word exploded in his head like a Roman candle, spitting sparks into his nerve ends. He never wanted to destroy so desperately in his life. All the years of fighting for medicine, and a place in the world of the healer ... they were wasted.

He now knew the phymechs weren't better than humans ... but how could he prove it? Unsubstantiated claims, brought to Calkins, would only be met with more intimidation, and probably a revoking of his license. He was trapped solidly.

How much longer could it go on?

Behind him, mechanical ears tuned, robot eyes fastened on the slumping, walking man. Rain was no deterrent to observation.

The murmur of a beater's rotors caused Bergman to look up. He could see nothing through the swirling rain-mist, but he could hear it, and his hatred reached out. Then: *I don't hate machines, I never did. Only now that they've deprived me of my humanity, now that they've taken away my life. Now I hate them.* His eyes sparked again with submerged loathing as he searched the sky beneath the climate dome, hearing the whirr of the beater's progress meshing with the faint hum of the dome at work; he desperately sought something against which he might direct his feelings of helplessness, of inadequacy.

So intent was he that he did not see the old woman who stepped out stealthily from the service entrance of a building, till she had put a trembling hand on his sleeve.

The shadows swirled about the shape watching Bergman—and now the old woman—from down the street.

"You a doctor, ain'cha?"

He started, his head jerking around spastically. His dark eyes focused on her seamed face only with effort. In the dim light of the illumepost that filtered through the rain, Bergman could see she was dirty and ill-kempt. Obviously from the tenements in Slobtown, way out near the curve-down edge of the climate dome.

She licked her lips again, fumbling in the pockets of her torn jumpette, nervous to the point of terror, unable to drag forth her words.

"*Well.* What do you want?" Bergman was harsher than he had intended, but his banked-down antagonism prodded him into belligerence.

"I been watchin' for three days and Charlie's gettin' worse and his stomach's swellin' and I noticed you been comin' outta the hospital every day now for three days ..." The words tumbled out almost incoherently, slurred by a gutter accent. To Bergman's tutored ear—subjected to these sounds since Kohlbenschlagg had taken him in—there was something else in the old woman's voice: the helpless tones of horror in asking someone to minister to an afflicted loved one.

Bergman's deep blue-black eyes narrowed. What was this? Was this filthy woman trying to get him to attend at her home? Was this perhaps a trap set up by Calkins and the Hospital Board? "What do you *want*, woman?" he demanded, edging away.

"Ya gotta come over ta see Charlie. He's dyin', Doctor, he's dyin'! He just lays there twitchin', and evertime I touch him he jumps and starts throwin' his arms round and doublin' over an' everything!" Her eyes were wide with the fright of memory, and her mouth shaped the words hurriedly, as though she knew she must get them out before the mouth used itself to scream.

The doctor's angry thoughts, suspicious thoughts, cut off instantly, and another part of his nature took command. Clinical attention centered on the malady the woman was describing.

"... an' he keeps *grinnin'*, Doctor, grinnin' like he was dead and everything was funny or somethin'! That's the worst of all ... I can't stand ta see him that way, Doctor. Please ... please ... ya gotta help me. Help Charlie, Doc, he's dyin'. We been tagether five years an' ya gotta ... gotta ... do ... somethin' ..." She broke into convulsive weeping, her faded eyes pleading with him, her knife-edged shoulders heaving jerkily within the jumpette.

126

My God, thought Bergman, *she's describing tetanus! And a badly advanced case to have produced spasms and risus sardonicus. Good Lord, why doesn't she get him to the hospital? He'll be dead in a day if she doesn't.* Aloud, he said, still suspicious, "Why did you wait so long? Why didn't you take him to the hospital?" He jerked his thumb at the lighted block across the street.

All his earlier anger, plus the innate exasperation of a doctor confronted with seemingly callous disregard for the needs of a sick man, came out in the questions. Exploded. The old woman drew back, eyes terrified, seamed face drawn up in an expression of beatenness. The force of him confused her.

"I—I *couldn't* take him there, Doc. I just couldn't! Charlie wouldn't let me, anyhow. He said, last thing before he started twitchin', he said, don't take me over there to that hospital, Katie, with them metal things in there, promise me ya won't. So I hadda promise him, Doc, and ya gotta come ta see him— *he's dyin', Doc, ya gotta help us, he's dyin'!*"

She was close up to him, clutching at the lapels of his jumper with wrinkled hands; impossibly screaming in a hoarse whisper. The raw emotion of her appeal struck Bergman almost physically. He staggered back from her, her breath of garlic and the slums enfolding him. She pressed up again, clawing at him with great sobs and pleas.

Bergman was becoming panicky. If a robocop should see the old woman talking to him, it might register his name, and that would be his end at Memorial. They'd have him tagged for home-practitioning, even if it wasn't true. How could he *possibly* attend this woman's man? It would be the end of his stunted career. The regulations swam before his eyes, and he knew what they meant. He'd be finished. And what if this *was* a trap?

But *tetanus!*

(The terrifying picture of a man in the last stages of lockjaw came to him. The contorted body, wound up on itself as though the limbs were made of rubber; the horrible face, mouth muscles drawn back and down in the characteristic death-grin called *risus sardonicus*; every inch of the nervous system affected. A slamming door, a touch, a cough, was enough to send the stricken man into ghastly gyrations and convulsions. Till finally the affliction attacked the chest muscles, and he strangled horribly. Dead ... wound up like a snake, frothing ... dead.)

But to be thrown out of the hospital. He couldn't take the chance. Almost without realizing it, the words came out: "Get away from me, woman; if the robocops see you, they'll arrest us both. Get away ... and don't try approaching a doctor like this again! Or I'll see that you're run in myself. Now get away. If you need medical aid, go to the phymechs at the hospital. They're free and better than any human!" The words sounded tinny in his ears.

The old woman fell back, light from the illumepost casting faint, weird shadows across the lined planes of her face. Her lips drew back from her teeth, many of them rotting or missing.

She snorted, "We'd rather die than go to them creations of the devil! We don't have no truck with them things ... we thought you was still doctors to help the poor ... but you ain't!" She turned and started to slip away into the darkness.

Faintly, before the rustle of her footsteps were gone, Stuart Bergman heard the sob that escaped her. It was filled with a wild desperation and the horror of seeing death in the mist, waiting for her and the man she loved.

Then, ever more faintly ...

"Damn you forever!"

Abruptly, the tension of the past months, the inner horror at what he had almost done to the blue-eyed girl earlier, the fight and sorrow within him, mounted to a peak. He felt drained, and knew if he was to be deprived of his heritage, he would lose it the right way. He was a doctor, and a man needed attention.

He took a step after her dim shape in the rain.

"Wait, I ..."

And knowing he was sealing his own doom, he let her stop, watched the hope that swam up in her eyes, and said, "I—I'm sorry. I'm very tired. But take me to your man. I'll be able to help him."

She didn't say thank you. But he knew it was there if he wanted it. They moved off together, and the watcher followed on silent treads.

CHAPTER SIX

The forever stink of Slobtown assaulted Bergman the moment they passed the invisible boundary. There was no "other side of the tracks" that separated Slobtown's squalor from the lower middle-class huts of the city, but somehow there was no mistaking the transition.

They passed from cleanliness into the Inferno, with one step.

Shadows deepened, sounds muffled, and the flickering neon of outdated saloon signs glared at them from the darkness. Bergman followed stolidly, and the woman led with resignation. She had a feeling the trip would be in vain. Charlie had been close to the edge when she had left, and this doctor's coming was an unexpected miracle. But still, Charlie had been so close, so close ...

They threaded close to buildings, stepping wide around blacker alley mouths and empty lots. From time to time they heard the footpad of muggers and wineheads keeping pace with them, but when the noises became too apparent, the woman hissed into the darkness, "Geddaway from here! I'm Charlie Kickback's woman, an' I got a croaker fer Charlie!" Then the sounds would fall behind.

All but the metal follower, whom no one saw.

The raw sounds of filthy music spurted out of the swing doors of a saloon, as they passed, and were followed almost immediately by a body. The man was thrown past the building, and landed in a twisted heap in the dirty gutter. He lay twitching, and for an instant Bergman considered tending to him; but two things stopped him.

The woman dragged him by his sleeve, and the gutter-resident flopped over onto his back, bubbling, and began mouthing an incomprehensible melody with indecipherable words.

They moved past. A block further along, Bergman saw the battered remains of a robocop, lying up against a tenement. He nodded toward it, and in the dusk Charlie Kickback's woman shrugged. "Every stiff comes in here takes his chances, even them devil's tinkertoys."

They kept moving, and Bergman realized he had much more to fear than merely being deprived of his license. He could be attacked and killed down here. He had a wallet with nearly three hundred credits in it, and they'd mugged men down here for much less than that, he was sure.

But somehow, the futility of the day, the horror of the night, were too insurmountable. He worried more about the fate of his profession than the contents of the wallet.

Finally they came to a brightly lit building, with tri-V photoblox outside, ten feet high. The blox showed monstrously mammaried women doing a slow tri-V shimmy, their appendages swaying behind the thinnest of veils, which often parted. The crude neon signs about the building read:

THE HOUSE OF SEX SEX SEX SEX!!!
AFTER SHOWS THE GIRLS' TIME IS THEIR OWN AND NO
HOLDS BARRED!
MORE THAN YOU CAN IMAGINE FOR A CREDIT!!!
LADY MEMPHIS AND HER EDUCATED BALOO—TRIX
DIAMOND—MLLE. HOT!
COME NOW, JACK, COME NOW!!

Bergman inclined his head at the poster blox, at the signs, and asked, "Is he here?" Charlie Kickback's woman's face greyed down and her lips thinned. She nodded, mumbled something, and led Bergman past the ticket window with its bulletproof glass and steel-suited ticket taker. The woman snapped a finger at the taker, and a heavy plasteel door slid back for them. The moment it opened, tinny music, fraught with the bump and grrrrind of the burlesque since time immemorial, swept over them, and Bergman had to strain to hear Charlie Kickback's woman.

He tensed, and caught her voice. "This way ... through the side door ..."

They passed the open back of the theater, and Bergman's eyes caught the idle twist of flesh, and the sensuous beat of naked feet on a stage. The sounds of warwhoop laughter and applause sifted up through the blaring music. They passed through the side door.

The woman led him down a hall, and past several dim grey doors with peeling paint. She stopped before a door with a faded star on it, and said, "He-he's in h-here ..." And she palmed the door open quietly.

She had not needed the silence.

Charlie Kickback would never writhe at a sound again.

He was quite dead.

Twisted in on himself, wound up like some loathsome pretzel, he lay on the floor beneath the dirty sink, one leg twisted under himself so painfully, it had broken before death. He had strangled to death.

The old woman rushed to the body, and fell to her knees, burying her face in his clothing, crying, namelessly seeking after him. She cried solidly for a few minutes, while Bergman stood watching, his heart filled with pity and sorrow and unhappiness and frustration.

This never would have happened, if ...

The woman looked up, and her face darkened. "You! You're the ones brought in them robots. We can't stay alive even no more, cause of them! It's you ... and them ..."

She burst into tears again, and fell back on the inert body of her lover. Her words fouled in her lips. But Bergman knew she was right. The phymechs had killed this man as surely as if they had slashed his pulmonary artery.

He turned to leave, and then it was that the follower leaped on him.

It had followed him carefully through Slobtown, it had immobilized the ticket taker in her suit, it had snaked a tentacle through the ticket window to keep open the door, and had tracked him with internal radex to this room.

Bergman stopped at the door, as the robocop rolled up, and its tentacles slammed out at him. "Help!" was the first thing he could yell, and as he did so, Kickback's woman lifted her streaked face from the dead man, saw the robot, and went berserk.

Her hand dipped to the hem of her skirt, and lifted, exposing leg, slip, and a thigh holster.

An acidee came up in her fist, and as she pressed the stud, a thin unsplashing stream of vicious acid streaked over Bergman's head, and etched a line across the robocop's hood. Its faceted light-sensitives turned abruptly, fastened on the woman, and a stunner tentacle snaked out, beamed her in her tracks.

As Bergman watched, the robocop suddenly releasing him to concentrate on the woman, the acidee dropped from her hand, and she spun backward, fell in a heap next to her dead Charlie.

Everything totaled for Bergman. The phymechs, the death of the thresher victim, the Oath, and the way he had almost shattered it tonight, the death of Charlie, and now this robocop that was the Mechanical God in its vilest form. It all summed up, and Bergman lunged around the robocop, trying to upset it.

It rocked back on its settlers, and tried to grab him. He avoided a tentacle, and streaked out into the hall. The punctuated, syncopated, stop beat of the burley music welled over him, and he cast about in desperation. Leaning against one wall he saw a long, thick-handled metal bar with a screw socket on its top, for removing the outdated light units from the high ceilings.

He grabbed it and turned on the robocop as it rolled slowly after him. His back to the wall, he held it first like a staff, then further down the handle, angling it. As the robocop approached, Bergman lunged, and brought fiercely his hatred to the surface. The club came down and smashed with a muted twanggg! across the robocop's hood. A tiny, tiny dent appeared in the metal, but it kept coming, steadily.

Bergman continued to smash at it.

His blows landed ineffectually, many of them missing entirely, but he struggled and smashed and smashed and smashed and his scream rose over the music, "Die, you bastard rotten chunk of tin, die, die, and let us alone so we can die in peace when we have to ..."

Over and over, even after the robocop had taken the club from him, immobilized him, and slung him "fireman's carry" over his tote area.

All the way back from Slobtown to the jail, to stand trial for home practitioning, collusion, assaulting a robocop, he screamed his hatred and defiance.

Even in his cell, all night long, in his mind, the screams continued. On into the morning, when he found out Calkins had had the robocop trailing him for a week. Suspecting him of just what had happened, long before it had happened. Hoping it would happen. Now it had happened, indeed.

And Stuart Bergman had come to the end of his career.

The end of his life.

He went on trial at 10:40 A.M., with the option of human (fallible) jury, or robotic (infallible) jurymech.

Irrationally, he chose the human jury.

An idea, a hope, had flared in the darkness of this finality. If he was going down, Bergman was not going down a coward. He had run long enough. This was another chance.

He meant to make the most of it.

131

CHAPTER SEVEN

The courtroom was silent. Totally and utterly silent, primarily because the observer's bubble was soundproofed, and each member of the jury sat in a hush cubicle. The jurymen each wore a speak-tip in one ear, and a speaker let the audience know what was happening.

Halfway up the wall, beside the judge's desk, the accused's bubble clung to the wall like a teardrop. Stuart Bergman had sat there throughout the trial, listening to the testimony: the robocop, Calkins (on the affair at the hospital, the day Kohlbenschlagg had died; the affair of the lounge; the suspicion and eventual assigning of a robocop to trail the doctor; Bergman's general attitudes, his ability to have performed the crime of which he had been accused), the old woman, who was Pentothaled before she would speak against Bergman, and even Murray Thomas, who reluctantly admitted that Bergman was quite capable of breaking the law in this case.

Thomas's face was strained and broken and he left the stand, staring up at Bergman with a mixture of remorse and pity burning there.

The time was drawing near, and Bergman could feel the tension in the room. This was the first such case of its kind ... the first flagrant breaking of the new Hippocratic Laws, and the newsfax and news sheet men were here in hordes; a precedent was to be set ...

The anti-mech leagues and the humanitarian organizations were here also. The case was a sensational one, mostly because it was the first of its kind, and would set the future pattern. Bergman knew he had to take good advantage of that.

And he also knew that advantage would have been lost, had he chosen a robot jurymech to try the case.

The nice things about humans tied in with their irrationality. They were human, they could see the human point of view. A robot would see the robotic point of view. Bergman desperately needed that human factor.

This had grown much larger than just his own problems of adaptation. The fate of the profession lay in his hands, and uncountable lives, lost through stupidity and blind dead faith in the all-powerful God of the Machine.

Deus ex machina, Bergman thought bitterly, *I'm gonna give you a run for your rule today!*

He waited silently, listening to the testimonies, and then, finally, his turn came to speak.

He told them a story, from the accused's bubble. Not one word of defense ... he did not need that. But the story, and the real story. It was difficult to get it out without falling into bathos or melodrama. It was even harder to keep from lashing out insanely at the machines.

132

Once, a snicker started up from the audience, but the others scathed the laughter to silence with vicious stares. After that, they listened ...

The years of study.

The death of Kohlbenschlagg.

The day of the operation.

Calkins and his approach to medicine.

The fear of the people for the machines.

Charlie Kickback's woman, and her terrors.

When he finally came to the story of the thresher amputee, and the calm workings of the phymech as his patient died, the eyes turned from Bergman. They turned to the silent cubicle where the jurymech lay inactive in waiting for the next case where an accused would select robot over human.

Many began to wonder how smart it would be to select the robot. Many wondered how smart they had been to put their faith in machines. Bergman was playing them, he knew he was, and felt a slight qualm about it—but there was more involved here than merely saving his license. Life was at stake.

As he talked, calmly and softly, they watched him, and watched Calkins, and the jurymech.

And when he had finished, there was silence for a long, long time. Even after the jurybox had sunk into the floor, as deliberations were made, there was silence. People sat and thought, and even the newsfax men took their time about getting to the vidders, to pip in their stories.

When the jurybox rose up out of the floor, they said they must have more deliberation.

Bergman was remanded to custody, placed in a cell to wait. *Something* was going to happen.

Murray Thomas was ushered into the cell, and he held Bergman's hand far longer than was necessary for mere greeting.

His face was solemn when he said, "You've won, Stu."

Bergman felt a great wave of relief and peace settle through him. He had suspected he would; the situation could be verified, and if they checked for what he had pointed out, not just blind faith in the machine, they would uncover the truth ... it must have happened before, many times.

Thomas said, "The news sheets are full of it, Stu. Biggest thing since total automation. People are scared, Stu, but they're scared the right way. There aren't any big smash sessions, but people are considering their position and the relation of the robot to them.

"There's a big movement afoot for a return to human domination. I—I hate to admit it, Stu ... but I think you were right all along. I wanted to settle back too easily. It took guts, Stu. A lot of guts. I'm afraid I'd have sent that woman away, not gone to tend her man."

Bergman waved away his words. He sat staring at his hands, trying to find a place for himself in the sudden rationale that had swept over his world.

Thomas said, "They've got Calkins for investigation. Seems there was some sort of collusion between him and the manufacturer of the phymechs. That was why they were put in so quickly, before they'd been fully tested. But they called in the man from the Zsebok Company, and he had to testify they couldn't build in a bedside manner ... too nebulous a concept, or something.

"I've been restored to full status as a surgeon, Stu. They're looking around for a suitable reward for you."

Stuart Bergman was not listening. He was remembering a man twisted up in death—who need not have died—and a blue-eyed girl who had lived, and an amputee who had screamed his life away. He thought of it all, and of what had happened, and he knew deep within himself that it was going to be all right now. It wasn't just *his* victory ... it was the victory of humanity. Man had stopped himself on the way to dependence and decadence, and had reversed a terrible trend.

The machines would not be put away entirely.

They would work along with people, and that was as it should have been, for the machines were tools, like any other tools. But human involvement was the key factor now, again.

Bergman settled back against the cell wall, and closed his eyes in the first real rest he had known for oh so long a time. He breathed deeply, and smiled to himself.

Reward?

He had his reward.

Repetitiously, the unifying theme to the stories in this collection is pain, human anguish. But there is a subtext that informs the subject; it is this: we are all inescapably responsible, not only for our own actions, but for our lack of action, the morality and ethic of our silences and our avoidances, the shared guilt of hypocrisy, voyeurism, and cowardice; what might be called the "spectator-sport social conscience." Catherine Genovese, Martin Luther King, Viola Luizzo, Nathanael West, Marilyn Monroe ... how the hell do we face them if there's something like a Hereafter? And how do we make it day-to-day, what with mirrors everywhere we look, if there isn't a Hereafter? Perhaps it all comes down to the answer to the question any middle-aged German in, say, Munich, might ask today: "If I didn't do what they said, they'd kill me. I had to save my life, didn't I?" I'm sure when it comes right down to it, the most ignominious life is better than no life at all, but again and again I find the answer coming from somewhere too noble to be within myself: "What for?" Staying alive only has merit if one does it with dignity, with purpose, with responsibility to his fellow man. If these are absent, then living is a sluglike thing, more a matter of habit than worth. Without courage, the pain will destroy you. And, oh, yeah, about this story ... the last section came first. It was a tone-poem written to a little folk song Tom Scott wrote, titled "38th Parallel," which Rusty Draper recorded vocally some years later as "Lonesome Song." If you can find a 45 rpm of it anywhere, and play it as you read the final sections, it will vastly enhance, audibly coloring an explanation of what I mean when I talk about pain that is

Deeper than the Darkness

A Folk Song of the Future

They came to Alf Gunnderson in the Pawnee County jail.

He was sitting, hugging his boney knees, against the plasteel wall of the cell. On the plasteel floor lay an ancient, three-string mandolin he had borrowed from the deputy, he had been plunking with some talent all that hot, summer day. Under his thin buttocks the empty trough of his mattressless bunk curved beneath his weight. He was an extremely tall man, even hunched up that way.

He was more than tired-looking, more than weary. His was an inside weariness ... he was a gaunt, empty-looking man. His hair fell lanky and drab and gray-brown in shocks over a low forehead. His eyes seemed to be peas, withdrawn from their pods and placed in a starkly white face. It was difficult to tell whether he could see from them.

Their blankness only accented the total cipher he seemed. There was no inch of expression or recognition on his face, in the line of his body.

More, he was a thin man. He seemed to be a man who had given up the Search long ago. His face did not change its hollow stare at the plasteel-barred door opposite, even as it swung back to admit the two nonentities.

The two men entered, their stride as alike as the unobtrusive grey mesh suits they wore; as alike as the faces that would fade from memory moments after they had turned. The turnkey—a grizzled country deputy with a minus 8 rating—stared after the men with open wonder on his bearded face.

One of the grey-suited men turned, pinning the wondering stare to the deputy's face. His voice was calm and uprippled. "Close the door and go back to your desk." The words were cold and paced. They brooked no opposition. It was obvious: they were mindees.

The roar of a late afternoon inverspace ship split the waiting moment, outside, then the turnkey slammed the door, palming it loktite. He walked back out of the cell block, hands deep in his coverall pockets. His head was lowered as though he were trying to solve a complex problem. It, too, was obvious: he was trying to block his thoughts off from those god-damned mindees.

When he was gone, the telepaths circled Gunnderson slowly. Their faces softly altered, subtly, and personality flowed in with quickness. They shot each other confused glances.

Him? The first man thought, nodding slightly at the still, knee-hugging prisoner.

That's what the report said, Ralph. The other man removed his forehead-concealing snapbrim and sat down on the edge of the bunk trough. He touched Gunnderson's leg with tentative fingers. *He's not thinking, for God's sake!* the thought flashed. *I can't get a thing.*

Incredulousness sparkled in the thought.

He must be blocked off by trauma barrier, came the reply from the telepath named Ralph.

"Is your name Alf Gunnderson?" the first mindee inquired softly, a hand on Gunnderson's shoulder.

The expression never changed. The head swiveled slowly and the dead eyes came to bear on the dark-suited telepath. "I'm Gunnderson," he replied briefly. His tones indicated no enthusiasm, no curiosity.

The first man looked up at his partner, doubt wrinkling in his eyes, pursing his lips. He shrugged his shoulders, as if to say, *Who knows?*

He turned back to Gunnderson.

Immobile, as before. Hewn from rock, silent as the pit.

"What are you in here for, Gunnderson?" He spoke as though he were unused to words. The halting speech of the telepath.

The dead stare swung back to the plasteel bars. "I set the woods on fire," he said shortly.

The mindee's face darkened at the prisoner's words. That was what the report had said. The report that had come in from one of the remote corners of the country.

The American Continent was a modern thing, all plasteel and printed circuits, all relays and fast movement, but there had been areas of backwoods country that had never taken to civilizing. They still maintained roads and jails, and fishing holes and forests. Out of one of these had come three reports, spaced an hour apart, with startling ramifications—if true. They had been snapped through the primary message banks in Capitol City in Buenos Aires, reeled through the computalyzers, and handed to the Bureau for check-in. While the inverspace ships plied between worlds, while Earth fought its transgalactic wars, in a rural section of the American Continent, a strange thing was happening.

A mile and a half of raging forest fire, and Alf Gunnderson the one responsible. So they had sent two Bureau mindees.

"How did it start, Alf?"

The dead eyes closed momentarily, in pain, opened, and he answered, "I was trying to get the pot to heat up. Trying to set the kindling under it to burning. I fired myself too hard." A flash of self-pity and unbearable hurt came into his face, disappeared just as quickly. Empty once more, he added, "I always do."

The first man exhaled sharply, got up and put on his hat. The personality flowed out of his face. He was a carbon copy of the other telepath once more.

"This is the one," he said.

"Come on, Alf," the mindee named Ralph said. "Let's go."

The authority of his voice no more served to move Gunnderson than their initial appearance had. He sat as he was. The two men looked at one another.

What's the matter with him? the second one flashed.

If you had what he's got—you'd be a bit buggy yourself, the first one replied. They were no longer individuals; they were Bureau men, studiedly, exactly, precisely alike in every detail.

They hoisted the prisoner under his arms, lifted him off the bunk, unresisting. The turnkey came at a call, and still marveling at these men who had come in—shown Bureau cards, sworn him to deadly silence, and were now taking the tramp firebug with them—opened the cell door.

As they passed before him, the telepath named Ralph turned suddenly sharp and piercing eyes on the old guard. "This is government business, mister," he warned. "One word of this, and you'll be a prisoner in your own jail. Clear?"

The turnkey bobbed his head quickly.

"And stop thinking, mister," the mindee added nastily, "we don't like to be referred to as slimy peekers!" The turnkey turned a shade paler and watched

138

silently as they disappeared down the hall, out of the Pawnee County jail-house. He waited, blanking fiercely, till he heard the whine of the Bureau solocab rising into the afternoon sky.

Now what the devil did they want with a crazy firebug hobo like that? He thought viciously, *Goddam mindees!*

After they had flown him cross-continent to Buenos Aires, deep in the heart of the blasted Argentine desert, they sent him in for testing.

The testing was exhaustive. Even though he did not really cooperate, there were things he could not keep them from learning; things that showed up because they were there:

Such as his ability to start fires with his mind.

Such as the fact that he could not control the blazes.

Such as the fact that he had been bumming for fifteen years in an effort to find seclusion.

Such as the fact that he had become a tortured and unhappy man because of his strange mindpower.

"Alf," said the bodiless voice from the rear of the darkened auditorium, "light that cigarette on the table. Put it in your mouth and make it light, Alf. Without a match."

Alf Gunnderson stood in the circle of light. He shifted from leg to leg on the blazing stage, and eyed the cylinder of white paper on the table.

It was starting again. The harrying, the testing, the staring with strange-ness. He was different—even from the other accredited psioid types—and they would try to put him away. It had happened before, it was happening now. There was no real peace for him.

"I don't smoke," he said, which was not true. But this was brother kin to the uncountable police line-ups he had gone through, all the way across the American Continent, across Earth, and from A Centauri IX back here. It annoyed him, and it terrified him, for he knew he was trapped.

Except this time there were no hard rocky-faced cops out there in the darkness beyond his sight. This time there were hard, rocky-faced Bureau men, and SpaceCom officials.

Even Terrence, head of SpaceCom, was sitting in one of those pneu-moseats, watching him steadily.

Daring him to be what he was!

He lifted the cylinder hesitantly, almost put it back.

"Smoke it, Alf!" snapped a different voice, deeper in tone, from the ebony before him.

He put the cigarette between his lips. They waited.

139

He seemed to want to say something, perhaps to object. Alf Gunnderson's heavy brows drew down. His blank eyes became—if it were possible—ever blanker. A sharp, denting V appeared between the brows.

The cigarette flamed into life.

A tongue of fire leaped up from the tip. In an instant it had consumed tobacco, paper, filter and denicotizer in one roar. The fire slammed against Gunnderson's lips, scaring them, lapping at his nose, his face.

He screamed, fell on his face and beat at the flames with his hands.

Suddenly the stage was clogged with running men in the blue and charcoal suits of the SpaceCom. Gunnderson lay writhing on the floor, a wisp of charry smoke rising from his face. One of the SpaceCom officials broke the cap on an extinguisher vial and the spray washed over the body of the fallen man.

"Get the mallaport! Get the goddamned mallaport, willya!" A young ensign with brush-cut blond hair, first to reach the stage, as though he had been waiting crouched below, cradled Gunnderson's head in his muscular arms, brushing with horror at the flakes of charred skin. He had the watery blue eyes of the spacemen, the man who has seen terrible things; yet his eyes were more frightened now than any man's eyes had a right to be.

In a few minutes the angular, spade-pawed, malleable-transporter was smoothing the skin on Gunnderson's face, realigning the atoms—shearing away the burned flesh, coating it with vibrant, healthy pink skin.

Another few moments and the psioid was finished; the burns had been erased; Gunnderson was new and whole, save for the patches of healthier-seeming skin that dotted his face.

All through it he had been murmuring. As the mallaport finished his mental work, stood up with a sigh, the word filtered through to the young SpaceCom ensign. He stared at Gunnderson a moment, then raised his watery blue eyes to the other officials standing about.

He stared at them with a mixture of fear and bewilderment.

Gunnderson had been saying: "Let me die, please let me die, I want to die, won't you let me die, please!"

The ship was heading toward Omalo, sun of the Delgart system. It had been translated into inverspace by a driver named Carina Correia. She had warped the ship through, and gone back to her deep sleep, till she was needed at Omalo snapout.

Now the ship whirled through the crazy quilt of inverspace, cutting through to the star system of Earth's adversary.

Gunnderson sat in the cabin with the brush-cut blond ensign. All through the trip, since blastoff and snapout, the pyrotic had been kept in his stateroom. This was the newest of the Earth SpaceComships, yet he

140

had seen none of it. Just this tiny stateroom, in the constant company of the usually stoical ensign.

The SpaceCom man's watery blue eyes swept between the pallid man and the teleport-proof safe set in the cabin's bulkhead.

"Any idea why they're sending us so deep into Delgart territory?" the ensign fished. "It's pretty tight lines up this far. Must be something big. Any idea?"

Gunnderson's eyes came up from their focus on his boot tops, and stared at the spaceman. He idly flipped the harmonica he had requested before blastoff, which he had used to pass away the long hours in inverspace. "No idea. How long have you been at war with the Delgarts?"

"Don't you even know who your planet's at war with?"

"I've been rural for many years. But aren't they *always* at war with someone?"

The ensign looked startled. "Not unless it's to protect the peace of the galaxies. Earth is a *peace*-loving ..."

Gunnderson cut him off. "Yes, I know. But how long have you been at war with the Delgarts? I thought they were our allies under some Treaty Pact or other?"

The spaceman's face contorted in a picture of conditioned hatred. "We've been after the bastards since they jumped one of our mining planets outside their cluster." He twisted his lips in open loathing. "We'll clean the bastards out soon enough! Teach *them* to jump peaceful Earthmen."

Gunnderson wished he could shut out the words. He had heard the same story all the way from A Centauri IX and back. Someone had always jumped someone else ... someone was always at war with someone else ... there were always bastards to be cleaned out ... never any peace ... never any peace ...

The invership whipped past the myriad-odd colors of inverspace, hurtling through that not-space toward the alien cluster. Gunnderson sat in the teleport-proof stateroom, triple-coded loktite, and waited. He had no idea what they wanted of him, why they had tested him, why they had sent him through the preflight checkups, why he was in not-space. But he knew one thing: whatever it was, there was to be no peace for *him* ... ever.

He silently cursed the strange mental power he had. The power to make the molecules of *anything* speed up tremendously, making them grind against one another, causing combustion. A strange, channeled teleport faculty that was useless for anything but the creation of fire. He damned it soulfully, wishing he had been born deaf, mute, blind, incapable of having to ward off the world.

From the first moment of his life when he had realized his strange power, he had been haunted. No control, no identification, no communication. Cut off. Tagged as an oddie. Not even the pleasures of being an acknowledged psioid, like the mindees, or the invaluable drivers, or the blasters, or the mallaports who

141

could move the atoms of flesh to their design. He was an oddie. A strange breed, and worse: he was a nondirective psioid. Tagged deadly and uncontrollable. He could set the fires, but he could not control them. The molecules were too tiny, too quickly imitative for him to stop the activity once it was started. It had to stop of its own volition ... and occasionally it was too long in stopping.

Once he had thought himself normal, once he had thought of leading an ordinary life—of perhaps becoming a musician. But that idea had died a-flaming, as all other normal ideas that had followed it.

First the ostracism, then the hunting, then the arrests and the prison terms, one after another. Now something new—something he could not understand. What did they want with him? It was obviously in connection with the mighty battle being fought between Earth and the Delgarts, but of what use could his unreliable powers be?

Why was he in this most marvelous of the new SpaceCom ships, heading toward the central sun of the enemy cluster? And why should he help Earth in any case?

At that moment the locks popped, the safe broke open, and the clanging of the alarms was heard to the bowels of the invership.

The ensign stopped him as he started to rise, started toward the safe. The ensign thumbed a button on his wrist console.

"Hold it, Mr. Gunnderson. I wasn't told what was in there, but I was told to keep you away from it until the other two got here."

Gunnderson slumped back hopelessly on the acceleration bunk. He dropped the harmonica to the metal floor and lowered his head into his hands. "What other two?"

"I don't know, sir. I wasn't told."

The other two were psioids, naturally.

When the mindee and the blaster arrived, they motioned the Ensign to remove the contents of the safe. He walked over nervously, took out the tiny trecorder and the single speak-tip.

"Play it, Ensign," the mindee directed.

The spaceman thumbed the speak-tip into the hole, and the grating of the blank space at the beginning of the tip filled the room.

"You can leave now, Ensign," the Mindee said.

After the SpaceCom officer had securely loktited the door, the voice began. Gunnderson recognized it immediately as that of Terrence, head of SpaceCom. The man who had questioned him tirelessly at the Bureau building in Buenos Aires. Terrence, hero of another war, the Earth-Kyben war, now head of SpaceCom. The words were brittle, almost without inflection and to the point, yet they carried a sense of utmost importance:

142

"Gunnderson," it began, "we have, as you already know, a job for you. By this time the ship will have reached central point of your trip through inverspace.

"You will arrive in two days Earthtime at a slipout point approximately five hundred million miles from Omalo, the enemy sun. You will be far behind enemy lines, but we are certain you will be able to accomplish your mission safely, that is why you have been given this new ship. It can withstand anything the enemy can throw.

"But we want you to get back for other reasons. You are the most important man in our war effort, Gunnderson, and it's tied up with your mission.

"We want you to turn the sun Omalo into a supernova."

Gunnderson, for the first time in thirty-eight years of bleak, gray life, was staggered. The very concept made his stomach churn. Turn another people's sun into a flaming, gaseous bomb of incalculable power, spreading death into space, burning off the very layers of its being, charring into nothing the planets of the system? Annihilate in one move an entire culture?

Was it possible they thought him mad?

What did they think he was capable of?

Could he direct his mind to such a task?

Could he do it?

Should he do it?

His mind boggled at the possibility. He had never really considered himself as having many ideals. He had set fires in warehouses to get the owners their liability insurance; he had flamed other hobos who had tried to rob him; he had used the unpredictable power of his mind for many things, but this ...

This was the murder of a solar system!

He wasn't in any way sure he *could* turn a sun supernova. What was there to lead them to think he might be able to do it? Burning a forest and burning a giant red sun were two things fantastically far apart. It was something out of a nightmare. But even if he *could* ...

"In case you find the task unpleasant, Mr. Gunnderson," the ice-chip voice of the SpaceCom head continued, "we have included in this ship's complement a mindee and a blaster.

"Their sole job is to watch and protect you, Mr. Gunnderson. To make certain you are kept in the proper, er, *patriotic* state of mind. They have been instructed to read you from this moment on, and should you not be willing to carry out your assignment ... well, I'm certain you are familiar with a blaster's capabilities."

Gunnderson stared at the blank-faced telepath sitting across from him on the other bunk. The man was obviously listening to every thought in Gunnderson's head. A strange, nervous expression was on the mindee's face. His glaze turned to the blaster who accompanied him, then back to Gunnderson.

The pyrotic swiveled a glance at the blaster, then swiveled away as quickly.

Blasters were men meant to do one job, one job only, and a certain type of man he became, he *had* to be, to be successful doing that job. They all looked the same, and Gunnderson found the look almost terrifying. He had not thought he could *be* terrified, any more.

"That is your assignment, Gunnderson, and if you have any hesitance, remember they are *not* human. They are extraterrestrials as unlike you as you are unlike a slug. And remember there's a war on ... you will be saving the lives of many Earthmen by performing this task.

"This is your chance to become respected, Gunnderson.

"A hero, respected, and for the first time," he paused, as though not wishing to say what was next, "for the first time—worthy of your world."

The rasp-rasp-rasp of the silent record filled the stateroom. Gunnderson said nothing. He could hear the phrase whirling, whirling in his head: *There's a war on, There's a war on. There's a war on*, THERE'S A WAR ON! He stood up and slowly walked to the door.

"Sorry, Mr. Gunnderson," the mindee said emphatically, "we can't allow you to leave this room."

He sat down and lifted the battered mouth organ from where it had fallen. He fingered it for a while, then put it to his lips. He blew, but made no sound.

And he didn't leave.

They thought he was asleep, The mindee—a cadaverously thin man with hair grayed at the temples and slicked back in strips on top, with a gasping speech and a nervous movement of hand to ear—spoke to the blaster.

"He doesn't seem to be thinking, John!"

The blaster's smooth, hard features moved vaguely, in the nearest thing to an expression, and a quirking frown split his ink-line mouth. "Can he do it?"

The mindee rose, ran a hand quickly through the straight, slicked hair.

"Can he do it? No, he shouldn't be *able* to do it, but he's doing it! I can't figure it out ... it's eerie, uncanny. Either I've lost it, or he's got something new."

"Trauma barrier?"

"That's what they told me before I left, that he seemed to be blocked off. But they thought it was only temporary, once he was away from the Bureau buildings he would clear up.

"But he *isn't* cleared up."

The blaster looked concerned. "Maybe it's you."

"I didn't get a master's rating for nothing, John, and I tell you there isn't a trauma barrier I can't at least get *something* through. If only a snatch of gabble. But there's nothing ... nothing!"

"Maybe it's you," the blaster repeated, still concerned.

"Damn it! It's *not* me! I can read you, can't I—your right foot hurts from new boots, you wish you could have the bunk to lie down on, you ... oh hell, I can read *you*—and I can read the captain up front, and I can read the pitmen in the hold, but I *can't* read *him!*

"It's like hitting a sheet of glass in his head. There should be a reflection or some penetration, but it seems to be opaqued. I didn't want to say anything when he was awake, of course."

"Do you think I should twit him a little—wake him up and warn him we're on to his game?"

The mindee raised a hand to stop the very thought of the blaster. "Great Gods, no!" He gestured wildly, "This Gunnderson's invaluable. If they found out we'd done anything unauthorized to him, we'd both be tanked."

Gunnderson lay on his acceleration bunk, feigning sleep, listening to them. It was a new discovery to him, what they were saying. He had always suspected the pyrotic faculty of his mind. It was just too unstable to be a true-bred trait. There had to be side effects, other differences from the norm. He knew *he* could not read minds; was this now another factor? Impenetrability by mindees? He wondered.

Perhaps the blaster was powerless, too.

It would never clear away his problem—that was something he could do only in his own mind—but it might make his position and final decision safer.

There was only one way to find out. He knew the blaster could not actually harm him severely, by SpaceCom's orders, but he wouldn't hesitate blasting off one of the pyrotic's arms—cauterizing it as it disappeared—to warn him, if the situation seemed desperate enough.

The blaster had seemed to Gunnderson a singularly overzealous man, in any case. It was a terrible risk, but he had to know.

There was only one way to find out, and he took it ... finding a startling new vitality in himself ... for the first time in over thirty years ...

He snapped his legs off the bunk, and lunged across the stateroom, shouldering aside the mindee, and straight-arming the blaster in the mouth. The blaster, surprised by the rapid and completely unexpected movement, had a reflex thought, and one entire bulkhead was washed by bolts of power. They crackled, and the plasteel buckled. His direction had been upset, had been poor, but Gunnderson knew the instant he regained his mental balance, the power would be directed at him.

145

The bulkhead oxidized, and popped as it was broken, revealing the outer insulating hull of the invership; rivets snapped out of their holes and clattered to the floor.

Gunnderson was at the stateroom door, palming the loktite open—having watched the manner used by the blaster when he had left on several occasions—and putting one foot into the companionway.

Then the blaster struck. His fury rose, and he lost his sense of duty. This man had struck him; he was a psioid ... an accepted psioid, not an oddie! His eyes deepened their black immeasurably, and his face strained. His cheekbones rose in a stricture of a grin, and the force materialized.

All around Gunnderson

He could feel the heat.

He could see his clothes sparking and disappearing.

He could feel his hair charring at the tips.

He could feel the strain of psi power in the air.

But there was no effect on him.

He was safe.

Safe from the power of the blasters.

Then he knew he didn't have to run.

He turned back to the cabin.

The two psioids were staring at him in open terror.

It was always night in inverspace.

The ship constantly ploughed through a swamp of black, with metal inside, and metal outside, and the cold, unchanging devil-dark beyond the metal. Men hated inverspace—they sometimes *took* the years-long journey through normal space, to avoid the chilling life of inverspace. For one moment the total black would surround the ship, and the next they would be sifting through a field of changing, flickering, crazy-quilt colors. Then ebony again, then light, then dots, then shafts, then the dark once more. It was ever-changing, like a madman's dream. But not interestingly changing, so one would wish to watch, as one might watch a kaleidoscope. This was strange, and unnatural, something beyond the powers of the mind, or the abilities of the eye to comprehend. Ports were allowed only in the officer's country, and those had solid lead shields that would slam down and dog close at the slap of a button. Nothing could be done, for men were men, and space was his eternal enemy. But no man willingly stared back at the deep of inverspace.

In the officer's country, Alf Gunnderson reached with his sight and his mind into the coal soot that now lay beyond the ship. Since he had proved his invulnerability over the blaster, he had been given the run of the ship. Where could he go? Nowhere that he could not be found. Guards watched the egress ports at all times, so he was still, in effect, a prisoner on the inver-ship. He had managed to secure time alone, however, and so with the captain and his officers locked out of the country, he stood alone, watching.

He stared from the giant quartz window, all shields open, all the dark-ness flowing in. The cabin was dark, but not half so dark as that darkness that was everywhere.

That darkness deeper than the darkness.

What was he? Was he man or was he machine ... to be told he must turn a sun nova? What of the people on that sun's planets? What of the women and the children ... alien or not? What of the people who hated war, and the people who served because they had been told to serve, and the people who wanted to be left alone? What of the men who went into the fields, while their fellow troops dutifully sharpened their war knives, and cried? Cried because they were afraid, and they were tired, and they wanted home without death. What of those men?

Was this war one of salvation or liberation or duty as they parroted the phrases of patriotism? Or was this still another of the unending wars for dom-ination, larger holdings, richer worlds? Was this another dupe of the Universe, where men were sent to their deaths so one type of government, no better than another, could rule? He didn't know. He wasn't sure. He was afraid. He had a power beyond all powers in his hands, and he suddenly found himself not a tramp and a waste, but a man who could demolish a solar system at his own will.

Not even sure he *could* do it, he considered the possibility, and it terrified him, making his legs turn to ice water, his blood to steam. He was suddenly quite lost, and immersed into a deeper darkness than he had ever known. With no way out.

He spoke to himself, letting his words sound foolish to himself, but sounding them just the same, knowing he had avoided sounding them for much too long:

"Can I do it?

"Should I? I've waited so long, so long, to find a place, and now they tell me I've found a place. Is this my final place? Is this what I've lived and searched for? I can be a valuable war weapon. I can be the man the men turn to when they want a job done. But what sort of job?

"Can I do it? Is it more important to me to find peace—even a peace such as this—and to destroy, than to go on with the unrest?"

Alf Gunnderson stared at the night, at the faint tinges of color beginning to form at the edges of his vision, and his mind washed itself in the water of thought. He had discovered much about himself in the past few days. He had discovered many talents, many ideals he had never suspected in himself.

He had discovered he had character, and that he was not a hopeless, oddie hulk, doomed to die wasted. He found he had a future.

If he could make the proper decision.

But what *was* the proper decision?

"Omalo! Omalo snapout!"

The cry roared through the companionways, bounced down the halls and against the metal hull of the invership, sprayed from the speakers, and deafened the men asleep beside their squawk-boxes.

The ship ploughed through a maze of colors whose hues were unknown, skiiiiittered scud-wise, and popped out, shuddering. There it was. The sun of Delgart. Omalo. Big. And golden. With planets set about like boulders on the edge of the sea. The sea that was space, and from which this ship had come. With death in its hold, and death in its tubes, and death, nothing but death.

The blaster and the mindee escorted Alf Gunnderson to the bridge. They stood back and let him walk to the huge quartz portal. The portal before which the pyrotic had stood so long, so many hours, gazing so deep into inverspace. They left him there, and stood back, because they knew he was safe from them. No matter how hard they held his arms, no matter how fiercely they shouted at him, he was safe. He was something new. Not just a pyrotic, not just a mind-blocked, not just a blaster-safe, he was something totally new.

Not a composite, for there had been many of those, with imperfect powers of several psi types. But something new, and something incomprehensible. Psioid + with a + that might mean anything.

Gunnderson moved forward slowly, his deep shadow squirming out before him, sliding up the console, across the portal shelf, and across the quartz itself. Himself superimposed across the immensity of space.+

The man who was Gunnderson stared into the night that lay without, and at the sun that burned steadily and high in that night. A greater fire raged within him than on that molten surface.

His was a power he could not even begin to estimate, and if he let it be used in this way, this once, it could be turned to this purpose over and over and over again.

Was there any salvation for him?

"You're supposed to flame that sun, Gunnderson," the slick-haired mindee said, trying to assume an authoritative tone, a tone of command, but failing miserably. He knew he was powerless before this man. They could shoot him, of course, but what would that accomplish?

"What are you going to do, Gunnderson? What do you have in mind?" the blaster chimed in. "SpaceCom wants Omalo fired ... are you going to do it, or do we have to report you as a traitor?"

"You know what they'll do to you back on Earth, Gunnderson. You know, don't you?"

Alf Gunnderson let the light of Omalo wash his sunken face with red haze. His eyes seemed to deepen in intensity. His hands on the console ledge stiffened and the knuckles turned white. He had seen the possibilities, and he had decided. They would never understand that he had chosen the harder. He turned slowly.

"Where is the lifescoot located?"

They stared at him, and he repeated his question. They refused to answer, and he shouldered past them, stepped into the droptube to take him below decks. The mindee spun on him, his face raging.

"You're a coward and a traitor, fireboy! You're a lousy no-psi freak and we'll get you! You can take the lifeboat, but someday we'll find you! No matter where you go out there, we're going to find you!"

He spat then, and the blaster strained and strained and strained, but the power of his mind had no effect on Gunnderson.

The pyrotic let the dropshaft lower him, and he found the lifescoot some time later. He took nothing with him but the battered harmonica, and the red flush of Omalo on his face.

When they felt the *pop!* of the lifescoot being snapped into space, and they saw the dark grey dot of it moving rapidly away, flicking quickly off into inverspace, the blaster and the mindee slumped into relaxers, stared at each other.

"We'll have to finish the war without him."

The blaster nodded. "He could have won it for us in one minute. He's gone."

"Do you think he could have done it?"

The blaster shrugged his heavy shoulders. "I just don't know. Perhaps."

"He's gone," the mindee repeated bitterly. "*He's* gone? Coward! Traitor! Some day ... some day ..."

"Where can he go?"

"He's a wanderer at heart. Space is deep, he can go anywhere."

"Did you mean that, about finding him some day?"

The mindee nodded rapidly. "When they find out, back on Earth, what he did today, they'll start hunting him through all of space. He'll never have another moment's peace. They *have* to find him ... he's the perfect weapon. But he can't run forever. They'll find him."

"A strange man."

"A man with a power he can't hide, John. A man who will sooner or later give himself away. He *can't* hide himself cleverly enough to stay hidden forever."

"Odd that he would turn himself into a fugitive. He could have had peace of mind for the rest of his life. Instead, he's got this ..."

The mindee stared at the closed portal shields. His tones were bitter and frustrated. "We'll find him some day."

The ship shuddered, reversed drives, and slipped back into inverspace.

Much sky winked back at him.

He sat on the bluff, wind tousling his grey hair, flapping softly at the dirty shirttail hanging from his pants top.

The Minstrel sat on the bluff watching the land fall slopingly away under him, down to the shining hide of the sprawling dragon, lying in the cup of the hills. The dragon slept—awake—across once lush grass and productive ground.

City.

On this far world, far from a red sun that shone high and steady, the Minstrel sat and pondered the many kinds of peace. And the kind that is not peace, can *never* be peace.

His eyes turned once more to the sage and eternal advice of the blackness above. No one saw him wink back at the silent stars. Deeper than the darkness.

With a sigh he slung the battered theremin over his frayed shoulders. It was a portable machine, with both rods bent, and its power pack patched and soldered. His body almost at once assumed the half-slouch, round-shouldered walk of the wanderer. He ambled down the hill toward the rocket field.

They called it the rocket field, out here on the Edge, but they didn't use rockets any longer. Now they rode to space on a whistling tube that glimmered and sparkled behind itself like a small animal chuckling over a private joke. The joke was that the little animal knew the riders were never coming back.

It whistled and sparkled till it flicked off into some crazy-quilt not-space, and was gone forever.

Tarmac clicked under the heels of his boots. Bright, shining boots, kept meticulously clean by polishing over polishing till they reflected back the corona of the field kliegs and, ever more faintly, the gleam of the night. The Minstrel kept them cleaned and polished, a clashing note matched against his generally unkempt appearance.

He was tall, towering over almost everyone he had ever met in his homeless wanderings. His body was a lean and supple thing, like a high-tension wire; the merest suggestion of contained power and quickness. The man moved with an easy gait, accentuating his long legs and gangling arms, making his well-proportioned head seem a bubble precariously balanced on a neck too long and thin to support it.

He kept time to the click of the polished boots with a soft half-hum, half-whistle. The song was a dead song, long forgotten.

150

He, too, was a half-dead, half-forgotten thing.

He came from beyond the mountains. No one knew where. No one cared where. *He* had almost forgotten.

But they listened when he came. They listened almost reverently, having heard the stories about him, with a desperation born of men who know they are severed from their home worlds, who know they will go out and out and seldom come back. He sang of space, and he sang of land, and he sang of the nothing that is left for Man—all Men, no matter how many arms they have, or what their skin is colored—when he has expended the last little bit of Eternity to which he is entitled.

His voice had the sadness of death in it. The sadness of death before life has finished its work. But it had the joy of metal under quick fingers, the strength of turned nickel-steel, and the whip of heart and soul working through loneliness. They listened when his song came with the night wind; probing, crying, lonely through the darkness of a thousand worlds and in a thousand winds.

The pitmen stopped their work as he came, silent but for the hum of his song and the beat of his boots on the blacktop. They watched as he came across the field.

There was no doubt who it was. He had been wandering the star paths for many years now. He had appeared, and that was all; he was. They knew him as certainly as they knew themselves. They turned and he was like a pillar, set dark against the light and shadow of the field. He paced slowly, and they stopped the hoses feeding the radioactive food to the little animals, and stopped the torches they boiled on the metal skins; and they listened.

The Minstrel knew they were listening, and he unslung his instrument, settling the narrow box with its tone-rods around his neck by its thong. As his fingers cajoled and pleaded and extracted the song of a soul, cast into the pit of the void, left to die, crying in torment not so much at death, but at the terror of being alone when the last calling came.

And the workmen cried.

They felt no shame as the tears coursed through the dirt on their faces and over the sweat shine left from toil. They stood, silent and all-feeling, as he came toward them.

Then with many small crescendos, and before they even knew it was ended, and for seconds after the wail had fled back across the field into the mountains, they listened to the last notes of his lament.

Hands wiped clumsily across faces, leaving more dirt than before, and backs turned slowly as men resumed work. It seemed they could not face him, the nearer he came; as though he was too deep-seeing, too perceptive for them to be at ease close by. It was a mixture of respect and awe.

151

The Minstrel stood, waiting.

"Hey! You!"

The Minstrel stood waiting. The pad of soft-soled feet behind him. A spaceman; tanned, supple, almost as tall as the ballad-singer—reminding the ballad singer of another spaceman, a blond-haired boy he had known long ago—came up beside the silent figure. The Minstrel had not moved.

"Whut c'n ah do for ya, Minstrel?" asked the spaceman, tones of the South of a long faraway continent rich in his voice.

"What do they call this world?" the Minstrel asked. The voice was quiet, like a needle being drawn through velvet. He spoke in a hushed monotone, yet his voice was clear and bore traces of an uncountable number of accents.

"The natives call it Audi, and the charts call it Rexa Majoris XXIX, Minstrel. Why?"

"It's time to move on."

The Southerner grinned hugely, lines of amusement crinkling out around his watery brown eyes. "Need a lift?"

The Minstrel nodded, smiling back enigmatically.

The spaceman's face softened, the lines of squinting into the reaches of an eternal night broke and he extended his hand: "Mah name's Quantry; top dog on the *Spirit of Lucy Marlowe*. If y'doan mind workin' yer keep owff bah singin' fer the payssengers, we'd be pleased to hayve ya awn boward."

The tall man smiled, a quick radiance across the darkness the shadows made of his face. "That isn't work."

"Then done!" exclaimed the spaceman. "C'mon, ah'll fix ya a bunk in steerage."

They walked between the wiper gangs and the pitmen. They threaded their way between the glare of fluorotorches and the sputtering blast of robot welding instruments. The man named Quantry indicated the opening in the smooth side of the ship and the Minstrel clambered inside.

Quantry fixed the berth just behind the reactor feeder-bins, sealing off the compartment with an electrical blanket draped over a loading track bar. The Minstrel lay on his bunk—a repair bench—with a pillow under his head. He lay thinking.

The moments fled silently and his mind, deep in thought, hardly realized the ports were being dogged home, the radioactive additives were being sluiced through their tubes to the reactors, the blast tubes were being extruded. His mind did not leave its thoughts as the atomic motors warmed, turning the pit to green glass beneath the ship's bulk. Motors that would carry the ship to a height where the driver would be wakened from his sleep—or *her* sleep, as was more often the case with that particular breed of psioid—to snap the ship through into inverspace.

As the ship came unstuck from solid ground, hurled itself outward on an unquenchable tail of fire, the Minstrel lay back, letting the reassuring hand of acceleration press him into deeper reverie. Thoughts spun, of the past, of the further past, and of all the pasts he had known.

Then the reactors cut off, the ship shuddered, and he knew they were in inverspace. The Minstrel sat up, his eyes far away. His thoughts deep inside the cloud cover of a world billions of light years away, hundreds of years lost to him. A world he would never see again.

There was a time for running, and a time for resting, and even in the running, there could be resting. He smiled to himself so faintly it was not a smile.

Down in the reactor rooms, they heard his song. They heard the build to it, matching, sustaining, whining in tune with the inverspace drive. They grinned at each other with a sweet sadness their faces were never expected to wear.

"It's gonna be a good trip," said one to another.

In the officer's country, Quantry looked up at the tight-slammed shields blocking off the patchwork insanity of not-space, and *he* smiled. It *was* going to be a good trip.

In the salons, the passengers listened to the odd strains of lonely music coming up from below, and even *they* were forced to admit, though they had no way of explaining how they knew, that this was indeed going to be a good trip.

And in steerage, his fingers wandering across the keyboard of the battered theremin, no one noticed that the man they called "The Minstrel" had lit his cigarette without a match.

About the Author

HARLAN ELLISON has been called "one of the great living American short story writers" by The Washington Post. In a career spanning more than 40 years, he has won more awards for the 74 books he has written or edited; the more than 1700 stories, essays, articles, and newspaper columns; the two dozen teleplays and a dozen motion pictures he has created, then any other living fantasist. He has won the Hugo award eight and a half times, the Nebula award three times, the Bram Stoker award, presented by the Horror Writers Association, five times (including The Lifetime Achievement Award in 1996), the Edgar Allan Poe award of the Mystery Writers of America twice, the Georges Melies fantasy film award twice, two Audie Awards (for the best in audio recordings), and was awarded the Silver Pen for Journalism by P.E.N., the international writer's union. He was presented with the first Living Legend award by the International Horror Critics at the 1995 World Horror Convention. He is also the only author in Hollywood ever to win the Writers Guild of America award for Most Outstanding teleplay (solo work) four times, most recently for "Paladin of the Lost Hour" his Twilight Zone episode that was Danny Kaye's final role, in 1987. In March (1998), the National Women's Committee of Brandeis University honored him with their 1998 Words, Wit & Wisdom award.